"Give me your hand."

Taking a deep breath, Reggie reached out to take Angus's hand.

"I need you to turn and wrap your legs around me."

"Nope. Not happening," she said, holding on to the tree with one arm, while squeezing his hand, his grip reassuring.

"Come on, I know you're tougher than that. You're a one-woman ranch owner, determined to make this ranch work."

"I'm tired. I can't do this anymore."

"Sure you can. You have a terrific kid who needs you." Angus tugged her hand, gently guiding her to him. "All you have to do is wrap your arms around me and hold on. Think of it as a great big hug. Come on. I know you've been wanting to."

Despite the desperate fear of falling to her death, Reggie couldn't resist the warmth of Angus's voice. God, she wanted to hug him right then and hold on to him for dear life.

HIGH COUNTRY HIDEOUT

New York Times Bestselling Author
ELLE JAMES

This book is dedicated to all the Army Special Forces soldiers
who've dedicated their lives and sacrificed so much
to protecting our freedom.

Recycling programs
for this product may
not exist in your area.

ISBN-13: 978-0-373-74915-7

High Country Hideout

Copyright © 2015 by Mary Jernigan

Printed in U.S.A.

Elle James, a *New York Times* bestselling author, started writing when her sister challenged her to write a romance novel. She has managed a full-time job and raised three wonderful children, and she and her husband even tried ranching exotic birds (ostriches, emus and rheas). Ask her, and she'll tell you what it's like to go toe-to-toe with an angry 350-pound bird! Elle loves to hear from fans at ellejames@earthlink.net or ellejames.com.

Books by Elle James

Harlequin Intrigue

Covert Cowboys, Inc.

Triggered
Taking Aim
Bodyguard Under Fire
Cowboy Resurrected
Navy SEAL Justice
Navy SEAL Newlywed
High Country Hideout

Thunder Horse

Hostage to Thunder Horse
Thunder Horse Heritage
Thunder Horse Redemption
Christmas at Thunder Horse Ranch

Visit the Author Profile page at Harlequin.com for more titles.

CAST OF CHARACTERS

Angus Ketchum—Undercover agent for Covert Cowboys, Inc. who lost his leg in the war in Afghanistan.

Reggie Davis—Ranch owner charged with keeping the ranch solvent for her son's inheritance.

CW Reinhardt—Last Chance Ranch's sixty-five-year-old foreman.

Jo Reinhardt—Last Chance Ranch's sixty-four-year-old cook and housekeeper.

William Coleman—Reggie Davis's brother and loan officer at the bank in Fools Fortune.

Lillian Kuntz—Real estate agent and Will's fiancée.

Dallas Faulkner—Real estate agent.

Hank Derringer—Billionaire willing to take the fight for justice into his own hands by setting up CCI—Covert Cowboys, Inc.

Theodore A. Davis Jr. (Tad)—Reggie's five-year-old son.

Kitty Toland—Reggie's friend and confidante.

Chase Marsden—Owns ranch adjacent to Reggie's. Friend of Reggie's late husband.

Chapter One

"Almost there, Ranger." Angus Ketchum shifted the truck into low gear and glanced across the seat at the German shepherd.

The animal sat patiently in the passenger seat as they bumped across the curving gravel road. Ranger stared out the window, taking it all in without comment. Angus envied the animal's calm. The fresh air and wide-open spaces would be good for the dog and hopefully for a washed-up soldier.

Before his last deployment he'd dreamed of owning or working on a place just like this. He'd loved fishing, hunting and working in the outdoors. Having grown up as a foreman's son, ranching was part of the cowboy he used to be.

Hard work, sweat, cattle and horses were what made his heart sing. He couldn't think of anything he liked better than riding the range; the quiet sounds of nature were all the music he needed.

When his father had retired from ranching at the ripe old age of fifty-five, Angus had been eighteen and on his way to Texas A&M University on a football scholarship. In the back of his mind, he knew he'd eventually come back to ranching when he could afford to buy his own spread.

His lips twisted as he applied the brake with his left foot. He'd joined the Corps of Cadets at A&M, graduated with a degree in engineering and joined the army as a brand-new second lieutenant.

Eight years and four tours to the Middle East later, his world had changed.

Gone was his goal of making a career out of the military and retiring to his own ranch. Gone was the dream of holding a decent job where he could pit his strength and intelligence against any challenge.

When he'd been discharged from the army, he had no idea what he would do, where he would go or how he would survive. Six months of surgery and rehab and he was out on his own.

If not for an old army buddy he'd met on his fourth tour to Afghanistan, he probably would have ended up drowning in a bottle of booze. He didn't feel as if he fit in the "real" world anymore. Things had changed. He had changed.

Chuck Bolton had given Angus's name to his boss with a recommendation to hire him.

Angus had laughed, telling Chuck he was a fool. But his friend had been insistent, and here Angus was, the newest member of Covert Cowboys Inc., for what it was worth.

What good was a broken-down cowboy to a ranch owner in Colorado? Ranching in Texas was hard enough, with drought, disease and rustlers. The hills and mountains of Colorado provided a whole different set of challenges for a cowboy, especially one with a bum leg.

His boss, Hank Derringer, must have seen something in him that he couldn't see himself. He'd hired him on the spot, without putting him through a thorough interview or physical evaluation. He'd gone on Chuck's word and Angus's military record, nothing else. He'd been a damned good soldier until his last tour, when everything had gone to hell. Now that he was out of the army, with no other job offers on his plate, Angus hadn't had any other option but to accept Hank's offer.

Before the warmth of their handshake had faded, Hank had given Angus his first assignment. Drive out to Fool's Fortune, Colorado, and go to work as a ranch hand for Reggie Davis on the Last Chance Ranch.

He'd almost laughed in Hank's face, but the man hadn't cracked a smile or clapped him on the back and told him he was kidding. Hank had given him an HK 40 handgun, a credit card and a pickup he could use as long as he was employed by CCI. All he had to do was to show up the next day for duty at the ranch.

Duty consisted of being undercover as a ranch hand while protecting the family.

Hank hadn't given him much to go on, stating he didn't have much himself. But when a friend of his had called for help, he'd promised to deliver.

His new boss assured him he could handle his mission. Glancing around at the rugged hills and valleys, with the Rocky Mountains as a backdrop, Angus wasn't as confident.

From what he'd seen so far since turning off the highway and crossing beneath the arched entrance to the Last Chance Ranch, the place was a large spread. It spanned the lower valleys and high foothills of the Rockies—rocky, rugged and more beautiful than any other place on earth. Angus hoped he could hack the terrain.

After the long drive, he was ready to get out and stretch. Phantom pain still shot through him, but he'd already exceeded the recommended daily allotment of over-the-counter pain meds by noon.

When he topped the next rise, the ranch house came into view. A sprawling log cabin sat in the middle of a field on a gentle knoll, with trees forming a windbreak around the structure. A huge barn stood behind the house, its exterior weathered a dull gray. Fenced paddocks stretched away on all sides, horses in one and a giant Hereford bull in another.

Pulling around the side of the house, he parked next to an old pickup that had seen better days and more paint.

A lanky, gray-haired man emerged from the barn, tugging the collar of his coat up around his ears. He paused and then trudged toward Angus's pickup.

"Stay," Angus told Ranger and climbed down. Careful to plant his good leg on the ground, he held on to the door of the pickup for balance as he got both legs underneath him. What a good impression he'd make if he fell flat on his face before he even shook the hand of the owner.

"Can I help you?" The older man shaded his eyes and stared up at Angus.

Angus stuck out his hand. "Angus Ketchum. I'm here about the ranch hand job."

The old man shook his hand, his eyes narrowing. "You the man Hank sent?"

"Yes, sir. You must be Mr. Davis."

"Nope," the old man replied. "Charles Wayne Reinhardt. Ranch foreman. You can call me CW."

"Is the owner around?"

"Not yet. Actually, I was the one who called Hank. He and I go back to our army days, a couple of decades back. The boss doesn't know you're coming."

Angus dropped the man's hand and stepped back, frowning. "I don't understand."

"Stuff's been happenin' around here. Accidents." CW snorted. "The boss doesn't seem to think there's a pattern. I do. That's why I called Hank. He promised I'd get a ranch hand that could help out with the work but also protect the family."

"Don't you think the owner should have a say?"

CW scraped the hat off his head. "The boss is stubborn. But then, you'll see what I mean soon enough."

"CW, is that our new ranch hand?" A gray-haired woman stood at the top of the steps to the wraparound porch on the log cabin.

"Yeah, Mamma. He's come all the way from Texas."

When Angus turned toward her, she smiled. "Well, come on in. I have a room all fixed up for you."

"You better go on up," CW said. "Jo will get you settled in. When you've dropped your gear, come on out to the barn. I could use a hand."

Angus nodded. "I'll only be a few minutes."

"Not if Jo has anything to do with ya." CW waved. "Go on. She's waiting. And remember, the boss can't know you're here to provide protection."

"Got it." Angus glanced toward his truck. "Do you mind if I let my dog out?"

The older man peered over Angus's shoulders at the dog sitting quietly in the front seat. "Does he chase cows or bark a lot?"

"Not that I know of. If I tell him to stay, he won't go anywhere."

"I guess that would be all right. Not sure how the boss will react, though." CW's brow remained knitted. "I don't have any patience with city dogs. All bark and trouble. Spooks the cattle."

Angus reached into the backseat of the four-door truck and retrieved his duffel bag. Then he snapped his fingers, and Ranger leaped out of the truck to the ground at his feet. When he walked toward the porch, the dog kept pace, glancing up for reassurance. Angus reached down to scratch the dog's head. He'd get him a bowl of water and some food as soon as he got settled.

Careful not to limp any more than he had to, Angus measured every step, wanting to prove himself capable without any preconceived handicaps. As he approached the steps, he was glad for his hard-core therapist, who'd insisted he relearn how to climb. He took the steps one at a time, placing his feet carefully.

Ranger walked up with him.

Jo held out her hand. "Hi, I'm Jolene, CW's better half. Everyone calls me Jo." As he shook her hand, she glanced at Ranger. "Not sure how the boss would feel about a dog in the house, but I guess it's better to ask forgiveness than permission, especially when the boss isn't around. Follow me." She led the way into the house.

The door he stepped through led into a large, airy kitchen with a ceramic-tiled floor, massive kitchen table and an oversize stainless-steel gas stove against one wall. Everything was neat and clean and the scent of coffee filled the air.

"I just put a pot of coffee on, if you're interested," Jo said. "You can drop your things in your room and come back through for a mug."

"As good as it smells, I'll wait. I'd like to get a feel for the place before sunset."

Jo led him through an open living room with a cathedral ceiling and an entire wall of windows facing the mountains rising up around them. The sun was on its way toward the peaks and would duck behind soon. Angus wanted to check out the barn and animals before it got too dark.

"This will be your room. We have a bunkhouse, but we haven't had a need for additional ranch hands since I came. Since there's only one of you, it would cost more to refurbish and heat the bunkhouse than to put you up in the big house. That, and with the troubles, CW and I thought it would be best for you to stay here." Jo pushed open a door. The room was spacious with rustic log walls. Centered on one wall stood a giant four-poster with a thick goose-down comforter spread across it and a quilt folded across the foot.

"I'll get a blanket for the dog to bed down on the floor," Jo offered.

"Thanks, but he has his own dog bed. I'll bring it in later. I promise he'll be no trouble. He's got better house manners than some people I know."

Jo laughed. "Good, because if he has any accidents, *you* get to clean up after him."

"Yes, ma'am." Angus liked the woman's candor and frankness. He dropped his duffel on the floor.

"The bathroom is across the hallway."

"Thank you, ma'am. Now, if you'll excuse me, I'd like to get outside."

"You bet. Supper is prompt at six o'clock. I'm making ham and beans, so don't be late."

The thought of a home-cooked meal warmed Angus's insides and he smiled. "I'll be there."

Jo gave him a serious look. "I'm glad you're here. The boss can't manage this big place alone. Especially with the troubles."

"What troubles are you having?"

"Accidents. Lots of accidents. A torn girth on a saddle…a loose floorboard in the loft of the barn…a gate hanging off its hinges. Hay bales falling off the stacks."

"Those sound like normal wear and tear on a ranch this size."

"It wasn't until the cut brake line that CW and I started putting two and two together. I'm not superstitious, and I don't believe a whole lot in coincidence." The woman planted her fist on her hip. "I've been here more than half my life. Things just aren't right. That's why CW and I decided it was time to call for some help."

"Fair enough." Although Angus wasn't sure how much help he'd be. "I'm here to do the best I can."

"And God bless you for it." She touched his arm. "I'd hate for anything to happen to the Davises."

Angus left through the kitchen and strode in his somewhat awkward gait toward the barn where CW had disappeared.

Inside, he waited for his eyes to adjust to the dim lighting from a dingy bulb overhead. He found CW mucking a stall.

"Grab a fork and get to work. I like to have the stalls clean before the boss gets back from the field."

"Does he need help out there?"

CW avoided his eyes. "Maybe tomorrow. It's getting late."

Angus found a pitchfork and went to work tossing soiled bedding into a wheelbarrow for transport out behind the barn to the compost heap. The scent of horse manure and hay brought back memories of his youth, the reminder so sharp and poignant it made his belly knot.

With every forkful of straw, his back strained and his leg throbbed, but he pushed on, enjoying the muscle strain and sweat.

Thirty minutes later CW checked on his progress. "I have to make a run to town for grain for the horses and to pick up the young'un. Anything you need?"

"Nothing I can think of except maybe a pair of work gloves." Having been in rehab for several months, his hands didn't have the calluses he needed for the kind of work he was doing. It would take time to build them up again.

He'd worked on strength, lifting weights and resistance training. But real, honest, hard work tasked so many more muscles than he remembered.

"I'll pick up some at the hardware store. When you get finished in here, there's a gate hinge that needs adjusting on the pasture fence, if you have time to get to it. Tools are in the tack room. Help yourself."

"Will do."

CW left, the silence a balm to Angus's soul.

He finished mucking the stalls and spreading fresh straw on the ground. Once he hung up the pitchfork, he headed outside in time to see the sun crest the peaks, the waning light lengthening the shadows from the surrounding hills.

Dragging in a deep breath, he filled his lungs with cool mountain air, the crisp chill making him feel more alive than he had in months.

As he released the air from his lungs, the bellows of livestock filled the air and a small herd of cattle appeared over the rise, a lone horseman riding at the rear, keeping the herd from straying too far to the right or left.

The rider appeared to be angling the cattle toward a holding pen in the corner of the pasture closest to the barn. With the setting sun at the rider's back all Angus could make out was a slender silhouette, guiding the animals home with a calm confidence only years in the saddle would produce.

He wondered how old the boss was or if he was just a small and wiry man. Handling a ranch and cattle required strength and stamina. No wonder he was having trouble and needed a ranch hand to help out.

Pushing aside his doubts about the boss's physical capabilities, when his own were in question, Angus angled toward the pen to see if he could help. He slipped through the wooden rails and waded through the cattle milling around waiting for the gate to open with the promise of being fed on the other side.

The rider nudged his horse toward the gate and leaned down to open it. Apparently the latch stuck and refused to open. Still too far back to reach the gate first, Angus continued forward, frustrated at his slow pace.

As the horseman swung his leg over to dismount, the gelding screamed, reared and backed away so fast the rider lost his balance and fell backward into the herd of cattle.

Spooked by the horse's distress, the cattle bellowed and churned in place, too tightly packed to figure a way out of the corner they were in.

The horse reared again. Its front hooves pawed at the air then crashed to the ground.

Unable to see the downed cowboy, Angus pushed forward, slapping at the cattle, shoving them apart to make a path through their warm bodies.

Afraid the rider would be trampled by the horse or the cattle, Angus doubled his efforts. By the time he reached him, the cowboy had pushed to his feet.

The horse chose that moment to rear again, his hooves directly over the rider.

Angus broke through the herd and threw himself into the cowboy, sending them both flying toward the fence, out of striking distance of the horse's hooves and the panicking cattle.

Thankfully the ground was a soft layer of mud to cushion their landing, but the cowboy beneath Angus definitely took the full force of the fall, crushed beneath Angus's six-foot-three frame.

Immediately he rolled off the horseman. "Are you okay?"

Dusk had settled in, making it hard to see.

Angus grabbed the man's shoulder and rolled him over, his fingers brushing against the soft swell of flesh beneath the jacket he wore. His hat fell off and a cascade of sandy-blond hair spilled from beneath. Blue eyes glared up at him.

The cowboy was no boy, but a woman, with curves in all the right places and an angry scowl adding to the mess of her muddy but beautiful face. "Who the hell are you, and what are you doing on my ranch?"

Chapter Two

Reggie Davis never got thrown from her horse. She prided herself in her horsemanship and ability to work long hours in the saddle without complaint or incident.

To be thrown in front of a witness and then tackled like a quarterback in a football game didn't sit well with her. Especially when she had no idea who the man was.

She scrambled in the mud to get her feet beneath her and stood. Then she stooped to snatch her hat off the ground, slapping it against her thigh. She'd have to let the mud dry before she could brush it off. Just what she needed, to be slammed into the mud by a big man with broad shoulders and ruggedly attractive features.

Her attacker rolled to his side and pushed to his feet, with a little help holding on to the wooden fence to pull himself upright.

When he straightened, Reggie's heart skipped a couple beats. The man towered over her. At five foot three with her boots on, that wasn't too darned hard. But it put her at a distinct disadvantage if the man decided to attack her again.

Knowing the best defense was a good offense, she crossed her arms, her boots planted wide, and glared up at the intruder. "Well? Are you going to explain yourself?"

His lips twitched and he bent to scoop his hat off the ground. "Next time I'll leave you to be trampled."

"I was doing fine on my own, thank you very much. Until you decided I needed a mud bath."

"Sorry, ma'am. A little mud can be washed off. A dent in the head won't wash out in a bath." He held out his hand. "Angus Ketchum, the new ranch hand."

Ignoring his hand, she kept her arms crossed. "We didn't hire a ranch hand."

"CW, the foreman, did. He said you needed a hand." Still holding his hand out for her to shake, he waited for her response.

She stared at him for a moment, refusing his outstretched hand. With the sun sinking quickly behind the mountains, the air chilled. The mud soaking her clothing cooled against her skin and she shivered. "I need to have a talk with CW. Don't start unpacking your bags yet."

"Yes, ma'am." He nodded toward the cattle. "Want me to get the herd into this pasture?"

Her eyes narrowed. "You ever worked cattle?"

"Most of my life."

"Then yes. Have at it." She stood back and waved a hand at the cattle now strung out, some heading back the way they'd come.

"First, let me get you out of harm's way." He grabbed her around the waist and she squealed, grabbing his shoulders as he lifted her to sit on the top rail of the fence.

"Don't ever do that again," she commanded, strangely breathless at the way his big hands had splayed around her middle and lifted her so effortlessly.

"I won't unless…you want me to." He winked, snagged her horse's reins, soothing him with murmured words of assurance. He ran his fingers over his neck and down to his hooves, checking them one at a time. "Can't see any injuries that would have caused him to rear like that." He glanced up. "I'll take him into the barn and give him a good going-over."

Reggie nodded, entranced by the quiet confidence and soothing manner the man displayed with the animal.

The cowboy led the gelding through the gate Reggie had been aiming for earlier and through the back door of the barn.

Reggie sat on the rail, letting her heartbeat return to normal.

A few moments later her cowboy reappeared

with a bale of hay, carrying it to the far side of the pen.

The man walked with a strange gait, limping slightly, more pronounced with the heavy bale in his grip.

As soon as the cattle spotted him and the hay bale, they raced through the gate, every last one of them, including Reggie's horse.

So, he knew what motivated cows. Anyone with half a brain would have figured it out. It still didn't give him the right to tackle her into the mud.

"They could use about five more of those, while you're at it," she called out. If he was applying for a position as ranch hand, he might as well feed the cows and save her the trouble. She still had her horse to curry, feed and stable, not to mention stalls to muck.

CW worked hard, but he was getting older and slower. After he'd thrown out his back last year, Reggie hadn't wanted him doing too much. By having him drive to town to pick up Tad from school, it made him slow down enough he wasn't killing himself with ranch work.

He'd been asking for a ranch hand for a while now. Reggie had finally agreed, unsure of where she'd come up with the money to pay one. But if she wanted to keep the ranch viable for her son to inherit one day, she had to have help.

The man reentered the barn and came out

carrying a bale in either hand, the limp much more pronounced, his jaw tight with the strain.

Show-off.

Not one to sit around while others worked, Reggie climbed down from the fence and almost stepped on a large dark creature. Her first instinct was *wolf*! She screamed and scrambled away. Her feet hit a patch of mud, slid right out from under her and she landed hard on her butt.

The animal stepped closer, its nose within biting distance of her face.

Reggie froze and then a long pink tongue stretched out and licked her chin, the dog whining its concern.

The ranch hand loped over to the fence and peered over the top to where she once again lay sprawled in the mud. "Are you all right?"

He started to climb over the fence, but she raised a hand. "I'm fine. I just wasn't expecting to be attacked."

The man's face split into a grin, his teeth shining white in the gloom. "Ranger is a highly trained purebred German shepherd and perhaps the most decorated dog in the US Army. He retired from active duty six months ago."

"Well, hooray for Ranger. Can you call him off me?"

"Ranger, sit." The man spoke softly and the dog responded immediately, squatting on his haunches.

Now that she knew it wasn't a wolf, Reggie felt stupid. For the second time that day she picked herself up and tried to dust the mud from her jeans. Ah, who was she kidding? They'd have to be hosed down before going into the washer.

Feeling bad for her nonchalance about Ranger's service, she reached out and scratched the dog behind his ears. In response, Ranger leaned against her leg and looked up at her with grateful eyes.

"Really tough, aren't you?" she muttered, a sucker for soulful eyes and fur. She slipped through the fence. "That hay's not getting itself out to the cows."

"Yes, ma'am."

"And stop calling me 'ma'am'. I'm not that old."

"Yes, ma'am."

She rolled her eyes. "What did you say your name was, cowboy?"

"Angus Ketchum." He held out his hand. "And you are?"

"Reggie Davis. The owner of the Last Chance Ranch."

In the darkness, she didn't miss his eyes flaring. When she took his hand, an immediate spark rippled up her arm and down her body. She had to look up at him to see his face, now shadowed in the dusk.

"You're the boss?" he asked.

"Yes. Me." She frowned and let go of his hand. "What? You don't think a woman can run a ranch on her own?"

"No, ma'am. I just thought the owner would be a man."

"Well, he was. A very good man, but he died last year. Now I run the ranch until my son is old enough to handle it himself. Do you have a problem taking orders from a woman?"

"No, ma'am." Angus held up his hand. "You're the boss."

"Damn right, I am." She slipped between the rails of the fence and strode across to where her horse was nosing his way into the herd, vying for a taste of hay. Snagging his reins, she led him into the barn.

Angus had gotten ahead of her and was carrying two more bales to the door. He paused and waited for her to lead the horse inside. In that moment, Reggie got a really good look at the man.

Dark hair, darker eyes and a chiseled jaw with the hint of stubble shadowing his skin. He certainly was handsome, in a rugged way. He sported dark smudges beneath his eyes and fine lines at the corners.

Yeah, he was handsome, but then, handsome wasn't always a good thing. She'd learned that most handsome men were too full of themselves to think of others. Angus would have to prove himself in other ways. Looks weren't everything. Honesty, loyalty and hard work were much more important in Reggie's books. It took a real man to make a cowboy, not just a cowboy hat.

She tied Jake's reins to a post and stepped into the tack room for a currycomb and brush. When she returned, Angus was loosening the girth on her saddle.

"I can do this," she said.

"I don't mind. It's my job."

"I can take care of my own horse," she insisted.

"Never said you couldn't. You take care of the horse. I'll take care of the saddle." He hefted the saddle and blanket and carried it to the saddle-tree in the tack room.

Having fended for herself over the past year, Reggie wasn't used to someone else taking charge. She tried to be ahead of CW as much as possible to spare him the additional work.

She couldn't lie; it was nice to have someone else carry her saddle to the tack room. After a long day out in the cold air and rocky hills, she was ready for a shower and sleep.

She'd be glad when her brother returned from his trip to Denver. The ranch was a lot of work. When he was there, it took some of the burden off her shoulders. Too bad he wasn't living there. Then again, she couldn't expect Will to spend all his time on a ranch he'd never own. As a Realtor, he needed to continue to build his clientele so that he could increase his sales and income. He'd been spending a lot of time with one of the Realtors in the firm he worked for. He'd gone with her to Denver for a seminar. Reggie suspected Will was falling for the woman. She'd met her once and hadn't really liked the woman, but then she might not have given her the benefit of the doubt.

Reggie brushed Jake from nose to tail, pausing to check his legs and hooves. The front leg had a long scrape on it, probably from when he'd reared.

Returning to the tack room, Reggie grabbed a tube of antiseptic cream, a clean rag and filled a bucket with fresh water. In a few short minutes she'd cleaned the scrape and applied the cream to the horse's leg. Then she took the time to work the tangles out of his tail.

Angus was outside for longer than she would have expected. When he didn't come back in for the last bale, she went looking for him.

As she stepped into the back doorway, he appeared, carrying what appeared to be a snake.

It rattled and Reggie jumped back.

Jake neighed and danced around, tugging at the reins tied to the post, his eyes rolling back in his head.

"What the hell?" Reggie demanded.

"Don't worry, it's not real. When I couldn't find an injury on your horse, I checked the ground where you fell." He turned it over and showed her the switch on the back that disengaged the rattling sound. "It makes the rattle noise when it senses movement."

"It's a toy?"

"Some toy." He glanced at the horse. "Do you have a bag we can put this in? Your horse has had enough trauma for the night."

Reggie retrieved a burlap sack from the tack room and helped Angus stuff the toy inside.

"You said you have a son?" he queried.

"I do. But that's not one of his toys."

Angus's lips tightened. "Is there anyone on the ranch who likes playing cruel practical jokes?"

She shook her head. "No. It's just CW, Jo, Tad and me. Sometimes my brother stays out here, but he'd never pull something like that."

"It's not a joke when someone almost got killed."

She frowned. "I wouldn't go that far. I was fine. I wouldn't have been killed."

"CW tells me there have been some unfortunate events around here lately."

Reggie shrugged. "CW is an old hen. He worries too much."

Angus tilted his head. "Could it be you worry too little?"

"What? So now you're an expert on what's going on at the Last Chance Ranch?" She glanced at her watch. "You've been here all of a couple hours and you're lecturing me." Reggie shook her head. "Unbelievable."

He stared at her for a long moment and then smiled. "You're absolutely right. Please accept my apologies." He set the bag with the snake aside, along with the previous conversation. "What do you feed the horse?"

Reggie accepted his retreat at face value and responded. "Sweet feed. It's in that container in the corner. Two coffee cans full."

Jake danced around the post she'd tied him to, his eyes wide, his ears pinned back. Reggie smoothed her hand down his nose in an attempt to calm the big animal.

When he settled, she led him to his stall, removed his bridle and hung it on a hook beside the stall door.

"Excuse me." Angus squeezed past her, accidentally brushing his body up against hers in the process. A bolt of electricity shot through her, leaving her fingers, toes and other odd places tingling.

At least, it appeared to be that the contact was an accident of the confined space. Surely the cowboy wasn't trying to get close to her on purpose. After she'd pretty much told him off, what man would flirt with her? And for that matter would she know if a man was flirting with her? She hadn't been on a date since high school, when she'd had what she'd thought was her last first kiss with her high school sweetheart, Ted. They'd been together all those years.

Angus dumped the feed cans into the trough and exited the stall, brushing against her again.

The sudden electrical surge powered through her body again and she hurried out of the way. Her husband had only been dead for a year. Surely that wasn't enough time to forget. Ted had been her world up until the day he'd slipped at the edge of a crevasse and fallen more than three hundred feet to his death. A year ago she'd been living the dream, working with her husband at her side, her son growing up in the most beautiful place in the world. One careless misstep and Ted was gone.

The past year had been an eye-opener. Sure, she'd helped a considerable amount while he was alive, but she'd also taken the time to be a mother to her young son. Tad had been four years old when his father died. He barely remembered the man, which grieved Reggie.

Her husband, Theodore Alan Davis Sr., had been a good man, and she'd loved him with all her heart. From high school in the small town of Fool's Fortune, they'd attended the same college in Denver and returned to help out on his father's ranch. When Ted's dad died, his mother followed soon after. They'd barely met their grandson, and Tad had never really gotten to know his grandparents.

The pain had faded, but the loss still left a hole in her life. Until she moved on, it would remain.

Seeing the new ranch hand move around the barn as though he knew what he was doing didn't help. This was Ted's barn, Ted's ranch, and Ted had been the love of her life. Why then, was she attracted to a man who'd knocked her on her face in the mud? Angry at herself, she turned away from the man who'd stirred in her something she wasn't ready to acknowledge. And all because of an accidental bumping of bodies.

"I'm going to the house for a shower," she said and left the barn. Better to step away than to continue to stare at the man. She'd have a word with CW. Maybe they could find an older or uglier guy to work the ranch. With that plan in mind, she headed for the house.

ANGUS'S LEG ACHED like crazy, but no matter how much it pained him, he'd die before showing even a shred of weakness in front of the owner of the Last Chance Ranch. Had he known the owner was female...what? Would he have refused the only job offer he'd had since being discharged from the army?

No. He couldn't. Who else would hire him?

His muscles clenched, his gut knotted and his heart rate kicked up.

Ranger nudged his fingers, reminding him to remain calm and to scratch his ears. The dog sensed when anger or anxiety threatened to over-whelm Angus. When it did, Ranger stepped in and nudged his hand or laid his nose in his owner's lap. The contact and resulting calm helped Angus regain his focus within seconds.

He had no problem working for females. He'd reported to female commanders. They were every bit as competent as the men, some more so. Then why did it bother him that Reggie Davis was female?

Because when he'd turned her over on the ground and stared down into those startling blue eyes, he'd taken a hit straight to his gut. The woman was everything he'd resigned himself to forget. She was strong, yet feminine and sexy as hell in blue jeans and a cowboy hat.

What woman would want a broken man like him? What did he have to offer? Crippled and plagued with PTSD flashbacks, he'd be more effort than he was worth. He wouldn't wish himself on anyone. Especially not a lone female trying to run a ranch all by herself. She didn't need the added burden.

The soft touch of her skin lingered with him, reminding him that he hadn't been with a woman since before he'd left for his last deployment to Afghanistan. Oh, there'd been doctors, nurses and physical therapists hovering around him for months, but that was different. They'd only touched him because it was their job, and he hadn't been in the least interested in them. How could he be? Up until he'd left rehab, and even now, he still experienced blinding residual and phantom pain from his injury.

His leg throbbed. He really needed to get off it and put it up for a while. He hadn't had to stand for hours in a long time. Working a ranch would prove difficult at best. But it beat sitting around feeling sorry for himself.

He found leather oil in the tack room and spent time oiling the leather on the girth straps and rubbing it into the saddle. The longer he waited, the less time he'd have to spend in the company of others.

Fifteen minutes after Reggie had left him in the barn, a door opened and closed. He sat quietly, hoping whoever it was would leave him alone.

From his position inside the tack room, Angus heard the shuffle of footsteps but couldn't tell who was there until a small boy appeared in the doorway.

He had longish dark brown hair, brown eyes and a pale little face. He must be the son Reggie had referred to, though he didn't look much like her.

For several long moments he stood, staring at

Angus rubbing oil into the saddle leather. "Are you a real cowboy?" he finally asked.

Angus glanced across at the boy. "I don't know. What is a real cowboy?"

The boy promptly answered, "A man who wears a cowboy hat and rides a horse."

Angus glanced at the cowboy hat sitting on the workbench beside him. "That's my hat."

The boy considered the hat and then Angus. "Do you ride horses?"

"Yes, sir."

"Then you must be a cowboy."

"I guess you have a point." Angus set the rag and oil aside and replaced the saddle on the saddletree. "Does your mother know where you are?"

The boy shrugged. "I come out here all the time."

"In the dark?"

He dipped his head. "No, but I know my way back."

"How about you and I go back together?"

The boy seemed to think about it and then raised his hand.

Angus captured the hand in his, marveling at how small and trusting the child was. Unused to small children, Angus held the boy's hand, swallowing the tiny fingers with his own.

"Have you had supper yet?" Angus asked.

"No, sir. Mrs. Jo asked me to come get you. It's almost six o'clock."

"Then we'd better get going or we'll be late for dinner."

They exited the barn together, Angus closing the door behind them.

"What's your name?" the boy asked as he walked alongside Angus, trying to match his short strides to Angus's longer ones.

"Angus."

"Angus." The boy tipped his head. "Isn't that a cow?"

Angus grinned. "A kind of cow."

Nodding, the boy trotted along a little farther before saying, "My name is Tad."

"Nice to meet you, Tad."

He had to admit, a strange feeling came over him as he walked with the boy at his side. It felt right. How, he didn't know. But he liked answering the boy's questions. The kid was polite, curious and instilled powerful protective instincts in Angus.

The child had pluck. He didn't ask Angus to slow down, taking three steps for every one of Angus's long, if gimpy, strides.

When they finally reached the porch, the boy ran up the steps and turned to face him. "Could you teach me how to ride a horse like a cowboy?"

"I could," he said, wondering what his mother

would say about him promising to teach the boy to ride.

As he mounted the steps, Angus's brows furrowed.

A woman, a kid and two old people on their own on a ranch in the hills. And someone had planted a snake where the woman was bound to ride. Although it was a fake snake, it had accomplished its mission. The horse had spooked, the rider had fallen. Whether it was a practical joke or had malicious connotations was pure conjecture.

CW seemed a pretty down-to-earth old man. He would not have called his old friend Hank for help if he wasn't convinced Reggie Davis was in trouble.

Angus's gut told him the situation bore watching. Even a man with only one good leg would be better than no one. But he would put in a call to the head of Covert Cowboys Inc. Reggie and her small son deserved someone more capable of taking care of them.

Chapter Three

Reggie had stripped in the mudroom, wrapped a towel around herself and headed through the house to shower. All the while her mind drifted back to the man in the barn and the way her body still felt after simply brushing up against him.

Naked beneath the towel, her breasts tightened. Jo and CW had insisted on the new ranch hand staying in the house. The older couple had a small cabin nearby, which meant they wouldn't be around at night should she need help.

What if she ran into him in the hallway when she was only wearing a towel?

Her body burned at the thought. Holy hell, she was lusting after a stranger. How could she, when her husband had only been gone a year?

She entered the master bedroom and closed the door. Riffling through a drawer, she unearthed clean underwear. If they happened to be her best, black-lace bikini panties, that was only because all her cotton underwear were in the wash.

Once in the master bathroom, she dropped her clothing on the counter and switched on the water, adjusting it to hot. When she faced herself in the mirror, she almost laughed out loud.

Though her body was somewhat clean, her jeans and shirt taking the brunt of the mud bath, her face was smudged with mud, some of it drying. Her hair stood on end, caked in mud. And to think, she'd been having lusty thoughts about the new ranch hand.

Covered in mud, she looked more like a pig in a poke than a young, beautiful and desirable woman. Not that she wanted him to desire her. No, sir. She was far from ready to reenter the dating pool. With a struggling ranch to run and a son to raise, she had her hands full.

Reggie stepped into the shower and eased beneath the hot spray. After a good soaking, she poured a heaping helping of shampoo into her palm and scrubbed her hair. Using a fresh washcloth, she scrubbed her face, arms and body and finally felt clean of mud and manure. And she smelled more like a woman than the horse she'd ridden in on.

Of course it was purely for personal hygiene, not a desire to prove she was an attractive woman beneath the jeans and dirt.

She stepped out onto the mat and dried off. She'd shared this bathroom with Ted. It was spacious, with a tub big enough for two people.

They'd shared many baths in that tub, learning to love each other, spending time together even after a hard day's work.

Their life together had been going so well. Why did he have to die?

A hard lump settled in her chest, but she'd already spent all her tears. The fact was, Ted was gone and she'd been left behind to take care of their son. If she could manage to keep up with the ranch his father had left for him. Ted's life insurance had paid off the land, now all she had to do was make the land support them.

And that was the biggest test of all. Raising cattle in the Rockies was iffy at best. The cold winters and the crazy amounts of snow made every day a challenge. If they lived closer to a city, Reggie could go to work and support them, but Fool's Fortune was so small. Most jobs consisted of selling real estate to the wealthy people from Denver and serving those wealthy people in the bars, diners and souvenir shops in town when they came to the mountains for vacations.

They'd been lucky so far this winter. The snows had held off. And a good thing, too, since the cattle had spread all up in the hills, and getting them down had taken Reggie longer than she'd anticipated. She still had a dozen in an upper pasture that needed to be brought down the next day. The weatherman was predicting the first blizzard before the end of the week.

For a moment Reggie debated adding a layer of foundation to her face and a little color to her cheeks. Shaking the thought from her head, she dabbed on lip balm and left the bathroom. In her bedroom, she threw on clean jeans and a cream sweater that covered everything. A glance in the mirror reminded her that while it covered everything, the sweater also hugged her body like a glove, emphasizing the curves of her breasts and hips. Maybe she'd be better off wearing one of the chambray shirts she worked in.

"Reggie, dear, supper's ready!" Jo called, ending the sweater debate.

As she hurried out into the hallway, she ran into a solid wall of bare muscle coming out of the guest bathroom. She braced her hands on a broad, naked chest and glanced up into deep brown eyes, so very different from Ted's hazel ones.

Strong arms came up around her waist, crushing her even closer to him.

"Steady there," Angus said, his chest vibrating with the deep resonance of his voice.

For a moment she forgot where she was as she inhaled the clean, woodsy scent of him, her fingers curling against his skin. He wore blue jeans and sneakers, and nothing else. The smooth expanse of skin drew her like a bee to honey, her insides igniting.

His lips curled upward on the corners as if he

knew the effect he was having on her. "Are you okay?" he asked.

"Mmm, yes, yes." When she realized her hands still rested against his bare skin, heat rose up her neck and filled her cheeks.

Reggie backed away. "I'm fine. Perfectly fine." She pushed a drying strand of hair away from her face and tore her gaze from his dark, enigmatic one. "Supper's ready and Jo likes everyone to be on time."

"So I've been told."

"Well, then." She smoothed that same strand again. "Well, if you'll excuse me—"

"Of course." Angus stepped out of her way and Reggie beat a hasty retreat to the kitchen.

What was wrong with her? She'd touched the man. Hell, she'd laid her hands all over his chest. And, damn it, she'd liked the feel of his skin against her fingertips. She had to pull herself together.

As she neared the kitchen she slowed, composed herself and stepped in.

Tad ran to her, his arms open.

She scooped him up and hugged him close. "When did you and CW get back from town?"

"While you were in the shower." He hugged her and wiggled out of her arms. "Did you meet the cowboy? He said his name is Angus. Isn't that a kind of cow? I like him. He's a real cowboy, and he's going to teach me to ride."

"Whoa, slow down there." Reggie laughed. "I was only in the shower a few minutes and you learned all that?"

He nodded and ran for the basket of bread rolls on the counter. "Jo made fresh rolls for dinner."

"I see that. Did you wash your hands?"

"Yes, ma'am." He held up his small hands. "See?" Then he darted around her and ran for the door to the kitchen. "Angus, you can sit by me. Where's Ranger?"

"He's resting in my room. I didn't think he'd be welcome at the dinner table." Angus winked as he stood in the doorway, wearing a clean, blue chambray shirt, buttoning the buttons as he stood there. When he finished, he took Tad's hand and let him lead him to the table.

"Sit there," Tad said, pointing to a chair.

"Tad…ask nicely," Reggie admonished.

"Please, sit there." He tapped the back of a chair and claimed the one beside it.

CW and Jo always sat at the other side of the table, which forced Reggie to sit at the end next to Angus. He pulled out the chair and waited for her to take her seat before sitting.

The table overflowed with food. After each platter had been handed around, Reggie lifted a forkful of ham and paused. "So, Angus, I'm not convinced we really need a ranch hand, but CW assures me we do. I can offer room and board, but I can't afford to pay a lot."

"I don't require a lot," he said, poking a bite of roll into his mouth.

"Then why would you want to work here?"

"I enjoy working with animals and being outdoors."

She studied him for a long moment. "You can stay." Reggie held up a finger. "On a trial basis."

"Fair enough." He turned to Jo. "Mrs. Jo, the rolls are wonderful."

Jo preened. "You look like you could do with some good old-fashioned home cooking."

The man was muscular, but his face was somewhat hollow, as though he'd been through rough times. Reggie raised her glass and drank a long pull of water, studying Angus in her peripheral vision.

Jo continued, "Since you're out here alone, I take it you're not married."

Water lodged in Reggie's throat and backed up into her nostrils. She stopped herself short of spewing it across the table as heat burned its way into her cheeks. Trust Jo to get down to the personal questions first thing.

ANGUS FOUGHT THE smile that threatened to erupt at Reggie's distress. The ranch owner turned an alarming shade of red and coughed several times.

He leaned back and thumped her on the back. "Are you okay? Don't need a hug, now, do you?"

"No…no…" she gasped. "Wrong pipe." Then

she glared across the table at Jo. "Leave Angus alone, Jo. He doesn't have to answer personal questions to work here."

Jo laughed irreverently. "He does if he wants another one of those rolls." She winked at him. "So, are you married?"

Angus liked the woman's forthrightness and laughing smile. "No, I'm not." And he probably never would be.

"That's interesting." Jo tilted her head. "A good-looking young man like you should already be settled with half a dozen children."

His jaw tightened. "The opportunity never came up."

"CW tells me you were in the army."

Angus's entire body tensed. "Yes, ma'am."

"Were you deployed overseas?" Jo continued her interrogation.

"Four times."

"Goodness. That would make it difficult to form a lasting relationship. Takes a special woman to marry a soldier and make it work." She glanced across at Reggie. "A strong woman who can keep the fires burning on the home front. Reggie's one of the most independent women I know. She can ride the range, round up cattle, muck stalls and still have time to read to Tad."

"Leave me out of this conversation," Reggie muttered and turned to Angus. "And watch her. She's an uncontrollable matchmaker."

"I am, and danged proud of it." Jo set her fork on the table. "Angus, you want another one of those rolls?" She passed him the basket.

Angus selected one and studied Jo Reinhardt. The woman obviously loved Reggie and wanted the best for her. She probably thought the young widow needed a new husband.

Too bad she was barking up the wrong tree.

His gaze shifted to Reggie. Her soft sandy-blond hair was drying, the curls springing up around her shoulders.

A man would be lucky to have her as his wife. She wasn't clingy or froufrou. Though she could ride and work animals like any other man, that was where the resemblance stopped. The way her sweater hugged her curves and her jeans caressed her hips, she was one hundred percent female.

"Got a lot to do tomorrow." CW's words pulled Angus back to the table.

The older man slathered his roll with butter. "Supposed to get down below freezing tonight. If the ground gets cold enough, that snow headed this way later this week will stick." He glanced at Angus.

Reggie nodded. "We need to get the rest of the cattle down from the upper pastures tomorrow."

Glad the conversation had shifted from him to the ranch, Angus took a bite of the smoked ham, enjoying the flavors.

"You up for riding so soon?" CW's gaze met

Angus's, making him wonder if Hank had told him the extent of his injuries.

Angus swallowed. "Yes, sir." He'd be damned if he showed a single ounce of weakness in front of Reggie. "It's been a while since I saddled up, but I'm sure I can manage."

CW continued to stare at Angus for a moment longer and then his gaze dropped to the buttered roll in his hand. "Riding a horse is a lot like riding a bicycle. Once you learn, it's easy to remember."

Angus hoped like hell CW was right. One thing he'd discovered in rehab was that, since his injury, he'd had to relearn everything to do with walking, running and riding a bicycle. Horseback riding would be an entirely different experience. He considered rising early to practice mounting without Reggie or CW standing around to witness his shame if it proved too difficult.

"Gonna be a bunch of stars out tonight," Jo said. "The weatherman reported there'll be a meteor shower today and tomorrow." She glanced at Reggie. "You used to love watching the meteor showers, Reggie."

"Really, Jo?" Reggie's lips twisted. "Not in frigid temperatures. Now, if you don't stop, you'll run off our hired help."

"What?" Jo held her hands up. "All I said is that there's a meteor shower gonna light up the sky. Tonight might be your only chance to view it."

Reggie finished her meal before everyone else and pushed back from the table. "If you will excuse me, I want to check on Jake's leg before I call it a night."

Angus pushed his chair back and started to stand. "Let me."

Reggie shook her head. "I can get this myself. Please, don't get up."

He waited until she'd slipped out the back door before he stood. "Need help with the dishes, Mrs. Jo?"

"No, thank you, Angus." Jo tilted her head toward the back door. "You go on out and help Ms. Reggie with that horse."

"Leave the kids alone, Mamma," CW said. "I know a boy who would love a couple of your chocolate-chip cookies."

"Me!" Tad raised his hand. "I want some."

The boy's delight at the cookies made Angus smile. To be so young and carefree that chocolate-chip cookies could make you happy was a gift. He slipped into his jacket and left through the back door, careful to let it close softly behind him. He thought about letting Ranger out for a walk, but didn't want to frighten Reggie again. He'd let him out later.

Reggie was nowhere to be seen, but a light

from the barn glowed like a beacon, drawing Angus across the yard.

Jo had been right about the sky being clear and the stars shining bright. Used to the big skies of West Texas, he did feel a little closer to the heavens in the higher altitude of the Rockies. And the air seemed cleaner, not dusty and dry like Texas.

For a moment he stood still, inhaling the fresh mountain air, for the first time in a long time glad he was alive.

Though Reggie hadn't asked for help, as the new ranch hand he felt obligated to check in with her and make certain she hadn't run into issues with the horse. And, based on his true job description, he was supposed to be keeping an eye on the owner and her family.

He turned and headed for the barn.

A scream rent the air, the sound coming from the direction of the barn.

Angus kicked out his bad leg and ran as best he could to the structure looming in front of him. As he neared the door, a shadow moved to the east of the barn. At first Angus thought it might be Reggie, but it slipped out of sight and a horse whinnied nervously from inside the structure, the sound of hooves banging against wood drawing Angus toward the barn door.

Had one of the animals broken out of a stall? Or worse, had Jake spooked again while Reggie had been in his stall? She could be lying at his feet, being beaten to death by flailing hooves.

Angus ran in his lumbering gait for the door and flung it open to a darkened interior.

"Reggie?" he called out, his pulse pounding so loud in his ears he was afraid he might not hear her response.

Reaching inside the door, he felt for and tripped the light switch. Nothing happened. Earlier, he'd noticed a flashlight hanging in a charger on the wall by the door. He felt along the boards until his fingers gripped the handle of the flashlight and he yanked it from its cradle.

Feeling as if he was taking far too long to check things out, he fumbled until he located the switch and turned it on.

Light sliced through the darkness.

Jake nickered worriedly and pawed at the boards of his stall.

Angus crossed to him and touched a hand to his nose. "Shh, boy. Where's Reggie?" He leaned over the gate and shined the light at the base of the horse's hooves. Nothing moved. All that was there was fresh straw.

The horse pressed his nose into Angus's hand.

"It's okay, boy. I'll find her." Angus turned around and pointed the light toward the door he'd come through, and slowly shone the beam across the floor. Nothing moved in front of the stalls. The floor was clean except for loose hay and straw.

As the beam slid toward the back of the barn it encountered a dark form lying in the shadows near the feed buckets he'd located earlier.

His heart beating hard against his ribs, Angus neared the lump. A few steps closer and he realized it was Reggie. Facedown, blood pooling beneath her forehead.

"Reggie, darlin'." He dropped to his good knee and braced his other leg out to the side.

She moaned and stirred.

"Reggie." He touched her shoulder. "Tell me you're all right."

She pushed against the floor and rolled onto her back, raising her hand to cradle the back of her head. "Ted?"

"Not Ted. It's Angus. What happened?"

"I'm not sure." She closed her eyes. "Something hit me in the back of my head."

Angus glanced around for a fallen object and found nothing. He recalled the shadow outside the barn and almost jumped up and chased after it. But with Reggie lying at his feet injured and possibly concussed, he couldn't leave her. Not with the distinct possibility that whoever had attacked her might come back to finish the job.

Chapter Four

Reggie stared up at the man leaning over her, blinking into a blinding light. "Do you mind not shining that thing in my eyes?"

"Sorry, darlin'." He placed the flashlight on the ground beside her and laid his hands on her leg. "Other than the back of your head, are you hurt anywhere else?" His fingers worked their way up her calf, knee and thigh, igniting a trail of electric tingles all the way.

Shocked at her body's response, she pushed his hands away. "I was hit in the head, not on the limbs."

"The fall could have caused more damage." He ignored her protests and swept his hands up the other leg and moved to her arms.

She stopped him just as his knuckles skimmed the side of her breast. "I said I'm fine, except for the splitting headache and overzealous first-aid care." Her blood hummed through her veins and places low in her belly came alive. Anxious to put distance between them, she sat up. "Really. I'm okay."

"Whatever you say, boss." He stood, collected the flashlight and extended a hand to her. When she hesitated, he shook his head. "It won't hurt to let me help you a little. Unless you're afraid. I promise, I don't bite."

"I'm not afraid." Nor was she in a hurry to touch the man whose hands had so easily stirred her blood.

"Well, you should be."

She frowned, the movement causing more pain to her already hurting forehead. "Why would someone purposely hit me?"

"Why would someone put a fake snake in your path?"

"I don't know. This is all ridiculous and too much like a conspiracy theory." She gingerly touched the lump rising on the back of her head. "Ouch."

"Are you going to take my hand or not?" He held it steady, daring her to take it.

Reluctantly she accepted his help and Angus pulled her to her feet.

Immediately, her vision blurred and she swayed.

His arm came up around her and he handed her the flashlight. "Hold this." Before she could protest, he shoved the light into her hands and scooped her up into his arms.

"Put me down!" She wiggled to free herself from his hold, but he refused to let go.

"You've had a head injury. Let me get to the house. We might need to call the doc."

"I tell you, I'm fine and I can get myself to the house." She clutched the light with one arm and held on around his neck with the other as he limped toward the house. "You can't carry me around. You're limping. Put me down."

His lips thinned and his hands tightened around her. "I can, and will, carry you to the house."

She could sense the unspoken words of *even if it kills me*. The tight set of his jaw and the determined look in his eyes made her still and let the man carry her, despite the lumbering gait and the slight hesitation when he reached the stairs.

One slow step at a time, he climbed the stairs, the lines deepening around his eyes and forehead. He was totally concentrated on getting her into the house.

"What's wrong with your leg?" she asked.

"Nothing."

"Look, you're my employee. If something should happen, I need to know what to expect."

"Not your concern. It won't affect my ability to do the work."

"Everything and everyone on this ranch is my concern." Damn, the man was stubborn. Almost as stubborn as she was. Reggie leaned down, twisted the knob on the back door and swung it open. "Especially when you insist on carrying me."

Without responding, Angus strode through the kitchen and into the living room, where he deposited her on the couch. "There, I'm not carrying you anymore."

Reggie opened her mouth to argue the point, but Tad entered the room, his eyes widening.

"Mamma?" He ran forward and stood in front of her. "You're hurt." He stared up at Angus. "Did you hurt my mamma?" His little fists clenched and he appeared to be ready to throw himself at the ranch hand.

"No, Tad. Angus didn't hurt me. I…fell and hit my head in the barn. Angus was good enough to carry me all the way into the house." She added the last part through gritted teeth, still unhappy about that particular fact.

The boy's face brightened and he hugged Angus's leg. "You *are* a cowboy."

Angus's face reddened. He quickly bent to loosen the boy's hold and held his hands as he stared down into the child's upturned face. "As the men in the house, we have to take care of the womenfolk. And right now, we need to wash the wound."

"I know where the bandages are. Mamma keeps them in her bathroom for when I have an owie." He ran from the room, his face excited.

Angus glanced down at Reggie. "I'll be right back, too."

"I told you, I can take care of myself." She started to rise.

Angus pressed a hand to her shoulder. "And disappoint your son when he's all set to take care of his mamma?" He shook his head. "Stay put."

Reggie didn't like taking orders from anyone, especially the stranger in her house. But the way he'd handled Tad and taken the opportunity to teach him to care for others made her sit back and accept the help.

"Fine." She crossed her arms. "For Tad."

Angus left the room and strode down the hallway to the bathroom. The sound of water running reached her ears, as did Angus's deep voice and Tad's childish one. Unable to hear their conversation, it was all she could do to remain on the couch. What was he saying?

Tad led the way into the living room, proudly carrying the box of bandages with cute little dinosaurs printed on them.

Reggie smiled. This was her little man. The spitting image of his father. Her heart swelled and she reached out to take his hand. "Thank you, sweetie."

"Angus is gonna clean the booboo and I'm gonna put the bandage on." He glanced up at Angus as if to confirm.

"That's right." Angus gave her son a serious nod. "It's an important job."

Angus leaned over Reggie and dabbed carefully at the cut on her forehead. Her senses picked up on everything about the man. The breadth of his chest…so close to her face. The bulging muscles of his arms in the blue chambray shirt…the trim width of his hips in the faded blue jeans. He smelled of leather and outdoors, the two scents she found most attractive on a man.

She closed her eyes to block out the cowboy, but she couldn't stop breathing. Each breath she took only added to her confusion. Why was she reacting to this man so much? She didn't even know him.

She had known Ted all her life. They'd practically grown up together in the same small town.

Angus had showed up out of nowhere. She knew nothing about him other than he was sensitive about his limp and didn't want her asking questions. What did he have to hide?

A little hand touched hers. "Does it hurt much, Mamma?"

She opened her eyes and smiled at Tad. "No, sweetie. I just didn't want to get anything in my eyes."

"All cleaned up. It's your turn, Tad. Remember to be careful not to get your fingers all over the white part." Angus leaned over him. "Here, let me show you." With his big hands, he helped the boy's little fingers open the individually wrapped package, peel the paper strips from the sticky adhesive and hold it out.

Together, they placed the bandage over the cut on Reggie's forehead. When the bandage was in place, she carefully felt the bruised lump.

"Well done." Angus stuck out his hand to shake Tad's.

Tad stood tall, his shoulders back, a serious expression on his young face. Then her son turned and hugged her. "Is it all better?"

"Yes, baby." Reggie returned the hug, her chest swelling with pride and an appreciation for the ranch hand who could have just done it all himself. Instead, he'd chosen to treat the event as a learning opportunity for her son.

Okay, so the man wasn't just an annoying addition to her ranch. He might come in handy. Tad could use more strong, male role models, since his father wasn't there to teach him certain things. Such as how to treat a lady.

Having shouldered most of the burden typically considered man's work, she hadn't really had the opportunity to teach her young son how to behave toward women. And he'd need those lessons in life as much as he'd need to know how to be strong, work hard and be accountable.

Angus backed away. "If you're sure you're okay, I'm going to check things out around the barn."

She nodded. "Be careful. I don't want you, uh—" her gaze shot to Tad "—bumping your head like I did."

He nodded and left the room.

As soon as she heard the sound of the back door closing, Reggie rose from the couch. "Come on, it's time for your bath and bed."

"Ah, Mamma. Can't I stay up?"

"You have school tomorrow and we have another chapter to read in your book about the ranch dog."

She held out her hand and Tad slipped his into hers. "When can I have a dog? Angus has one."

"When you're old enough to take care of one all by yourself."

"I'm old enough. I took care of you," he pointed out.

She ruffled his hair. "Yes, you did. I'll think about it."

He skipped along beside her. "Can I name the dog Ranger?"

"We haven't got one yet. Besides, Angus's dog is named Ranger. Don't you think you should give a dog his very own name?"

The conversation continued as it usually did, with Tad asking questions and making observations that surprised her at his level of maturity for a five-year old.

Reggie herded Tad through his bath, allowing him to play for a while before bundling him in a warm towel and clean pajamas. After he brushed his teeth, he climbed into his little bed and waited for her to read to him. This was one thing she'd always insisted on, even after Ted's passing. Some things had to remain consistent to keep Tad on track with growing up normal and well-adjusted.

She settled on the edge of his bed, opened the book to the chapter she'd stopped at the previous night and read.

ANGUS TOOK RANGER outside with him and spent time circling the barn, searching for some indication of who had been inside and hit Reggie in the head. If he hadn't been sure before, he was certain now. Someone was targeting Reggie. She needed protection. Perhaps he wasn't the one to provide it. Why had Hank insisted he was the man for the job?

As he shone the flashlight at the ground around the exterior of the barn, phantom pain burst like a firecracker, shooting up his leg and throughout his body. He stopped for a moment and clenched his jaw until the pain eased.

Pushing aside the residual pain, he concentrated on the ground, searching for footprints. The ground was hard-packed except near the rear of the barn, where he'd hosed out the wheelbarrow earlier. Footprints made inch-deep wells in the mud. He set off in the direction they were heading and found a couple more. They were smaller than his own, but then, he was a big guy.

The trail led over the top of a small hill and down to a gravel road on the other side. It was not much more than a dirt path. He followed it to where it connected with the road leading up to the ranch. At the junction, he could see fresh tire tracks in the loose dirt. They were narrow and knobby, like those of a four-wheeler, and the direction they were heading was back toward town. Near the tracks, almost hidden by a bush, he found a four-foot length of weathered two-by-four with a smear of blood on it. His gut knotted as he lifted the board out of the brush.

Following the road much farther wouldn't gain him anything. The best he could hope for was to make a trip to Fool's Fortune the next day and do some nosing around. He wished he had the ability to lift prints from the board. Perhaps whoever had hit Reggie was in some criminal database. Hank might have connections.

In the meantime he needed to get back to the house and stay close to the family he was there to protect, in case Reggie's attacker decided to return in the middle of the night.

Once inside, he shed his jacket and hung it on a hook on the wall beside the kitchen door. Though his leg ached and he needed to elevate it, he couldn't until he felt confident Reggie and her son were okay. He spent time checking door and window locks and shooting the dead bolts home. They might have felt comfortable leaving doors unlocked in the past, but times had changed.

Reassured all the locks were in place, Angus headed down the hallway to his bedroom. As he passed an open door, he heard Reggie's voice speaking softly.

He paused, liking this gentle side of the woman who'd been tough as nails since he'd arrived. Curious, he leaned through the doorway.

Reggie sat on the side of a twin-size bed covered with a quilt decorated with pictures of cowboy hats, cowboy boots, lassos and spurs. Tad lay beneath it, his head resting against the pillow, his eyes half closed.

"'Poke, the ranch dog, barked at the bull, until the bull backed away from the boy.'"

"Poke wasn't afraid, was he?" Tad mumbled sleepily.

"No, he wasn't. He protected his boy from the bull."

"When I get my dog, I'll name him Poke." Tad yawned and rolled onto his side, tucking his hand beneath his chin. "Until I get my own dog, do you think Angus would let me pet Ranger?"

"You need to ask Angus. Ranger was an army dog. He might not be used to little kids."

"I'll ask Angus in the morning." Tad yawned again and closed his eyes. "Will you tell him to tuck me in when he comes back in?"

"I read you a book, but you'd rather have Angus tuck you in?" Reggie leaned over and kissed his cheek. "I'll tell him. I love you, baby."

"I love you, too." Tad's voice faded as he nestled into the blanket.

Reggie pulled the quilt up beneath his chin and stared down at the boy a few moments longer, love shining from her eyes.

Angus backed away from the doorway as quietly as he could and walked toward the kitchen, feeling as though he'd violated a private moment between Reggie and her son. But he wasn't sorry he had.

The image of the tough ranch owner tucking her kid in like any loving mother would was seared into Angus's mind. The woman had enough on her plate that she didn't need to be plagued by some idiot trying to hurt her, or worse, kill her.

Anger boiled beneath the surface as Angus hovered in the kitchen long enough that Reggie wouldn't suspect he'd been spying on her.

When he'd waited what he thought was enough time, he walked out of the kitchen and right into Reggie. His arms came up around her automatically to steady them both.

She squealed and braced her hands on his chest.

Angus chuckled. "This is becoming a habit." Though neither one of them was at risk for falling, he was reluctant to let go of her. Her warm, soft body pressed against his was too tempting. She smelled like honeysuckle, bringing back memories of his happy childhood on a ranch in Texas.

"Anyone ever tell you that your hair is the color of hay?" he said before he could stop himself.

"Most women might count that as an insult," she said, her voice a little breathless, probably from having been surprised by him.

"I think the color of hay is beautiful and that it represents stability and a plentiful harvest."

Reggie smiled. "My thoughts exactly. So I'll take your comment as a compliment."

"As you should."

Her back stiffened. "I believe I can stand on my own."

"I know," he said, staring into the prettiest blue eyes he could remember looking into. He wanted to tell her that, too, but he figured, following his last compliment, it might be too much, coming from a ranch hand. God, she smelled like home.

"You can let go of me now."

He shook his head. "Sorry, darlin'." Before he could think past the consequences, he cupped the back of her head and leaned in, his lips hovering over hers. "For some reason, I can't seem to." He wanted to kiss her, but more than that, he wanted her to *want* to kiss him. Instead of taking her lips, he left it up to her. His breath caught and held, waiting for her response.

For a moment she stiffened, her eyes widening. Her gaze shifted from his eyes to his lips. Then she melted against him and stood on her toes to close the distance, pressing her lips to his.

Once she did, there was no going back for Angus. He deepened the kiss, sweeping his tongue in to claim hers in a long sensuous glide. She tasted of minty toothpaste, clean, fresh and sexy as hell.

Her fingers curled into his shirt and dragged him closer.

Angus's hands slipped low on her back, holding her against the hard ridge of his arousal. At that moment he wanted this woman more than he'd wanted anything in his life. He slipped his hands down over her bottom and started to lift her—and a lightning bolt of pain ripped up his leg. He broke the kiss, sucking in a sharp breath and clenching his jaw to keep from yelling out.

"What's wrong?" Reggie's hand rested on his chest, her gaze on his face. "Did I hurt you?"

"No." He pushed her to arm's length. "I just… can't…" He dropped his hands to his sides and backed away, limping more noticeably. "I shouldn't have done that. I'm sorry. It won't happen again."

Her kiss-swollen lips pressed into a tight line.

"I'm just as at fault, but I can assure you, it won't happen again." She turned to walk away.

Angus doubled over. He hadn't felt an attack this strong in weeks and he struggled to beat it back. Hiding his pain was a losing proposition, but Angus bit down hard, refusing to show weakness.

Reggie stopped and turned back.

Angus straightened immediately, his stomach tightening.

Reggie stared at him for a minute, her eyes narrowing. Finally she sighed, "Tad wanted you to tuck him in. Don't feel like you have to. He's probably already asleep anyway." With those parting words, she left him standing in the kitchen, alone with nothing but his pain as a reminder of all he'd lost.

Chapter Five

Reggie swallowed a couple of painkillers to dull the throbbing on her bruised forehead and lay awake half the night anyway.

What had happened in the kitchen between her and the new ranch hand? Had she completely lost her mind?

He'd given her the option to break away, to tell him she didn't *want* to kiss him. Hell, to do anything but what she'd ended up doing. Instead she'd kissed him, full-on, in a tongue-twisting, lost-in-the-moment meeting of the mouths.

Once she finally slipped into sleep, she dreamed she was with Ted. That he was alive and holding her in his arms as he had on their wedding night. In the dream, he kissed her…but when he pulled away, his was not the face she saw. In Ted's place was the ruggedly handsome Angus, his eyes shadowed with pain.

Reggie woke with a start, her heart beating so fast she thought she might be having a heart attack. She looked around at the room she'd shared with her husband, the moonlight shining through the windows. For a moment she thought she saw Ted standing at the end of her bed. When she blinked, he was gone.

She rolled over, hugging her pillow, alone in her bed. She prayed for tears, but they wouldn't come. She'd cried all her tears for Ted. She couldn't cry anymore. He was gone, and she was alive and feeling needs she would rather not feel.

After a long time she fell back to sleep, waking with her alarm rather than before it as she usually did.

Tired from her restless night's sleep, she jumped into a cool shower to wake her and then went into Tad's room to get him up and ready for school.

It was the same old routine, but one she loved doing. He always made Reggie glad she'd kept going when Ted had died. He was worth it all.

Tad wasn't in his bed.

A moment of panic hit her and she hurried along the hall to the kitchen, following the sounds of voices and laughter.

Jo stood at the stove, cooking breakfast. Angus and Tad were busy setting the table with clean cutlery and glasses.

"Mamma, look at what I did." He pointed to the table. "I set out the forks and spoons. Angus set out the knives." He turned to the corner. "And

Ranger is being good sitting in the corner. Angus said I could pet him as long as he was around."

Reggie swallowed her irritation that Angus seemed well rested and cheerful when her sleep had been so…disturbed.

CW entered the kitchen. "Something smells good." He slipped his arms around Jo and sniffed her neck. "Ah, I should have known it was you."

"Silly man." Jo waved the spatula at her husband. "Not in front of the young'uns."

"What? Surely they've seen a man love on his woman before." He gave her a loud, smacking kiss and turned to wink at Reggie and Tad. "How about some scrambled eggs and waffles?"

Tad clapped his hands. "Waffles, please. Can you make an extra one for Ranger?"

Reggie frowned. "Angus might not want Ranger to eat people food."

Tad's eyes rounded. "But waffles are the best."

"And I'm sure Ranger would love it, but he's on a strict diet to keep him healthy." Angus leaned close to Tad. "But if you want to sneak him one little bite, I'm sure he'd be your friend forever."

"Just one bite, Tad," Reggie said. "You don't want Ranger to get sick."

Tad shook his head, his eyes wide. "No, I don't."

As soon as breakfast was served, Tad broke off

a corner of his waffle and looked from Reggie to Angus. "Now?"

Reggie nodded toward Angus. "It's up to Angus."

"You need to hold it like this." Angus held out his hand, palm up, fingers together.

Tad hopped out of his chair and walked to the dog.

Reggie watched closely. The dog, as big as the boy, could rip his face off in one bite. "What did Ranger do in the military?"

"He was a sniffing dog. He could find drugs, explosives," his voice dropped lower so that only Reggie would hear, "and human remains."

A chill rippled across Reggie's skin. "At least he wasn't an attack dog."

"No. I wouldn't have asked you to take him in with me if he was dangerous. Truth is, he was getting old, his hips aren't what they used to be, and it was either find him a home or put him down."

"Such a shame to put a good dog like that down just because his body doesn't work as well as it used to," Reggie said.

Angus's lips thinned. "I felt the same. Now he's my companion, and I couldn't ask for a better one."

"I can see he means a lot to you."

Tad held out his hand just as Angus had

showed him and placed the waffle in the middle of his palm.

Angus spoke to Ranger. "It's okay."

The dog glanced from Angus to Tad and sniffed tentatively. Then he snaked out his long pink tongue and licked the waffle out of Tad's hand.

Tad giggled, wiped his palm on his jeans and said, "He likes it!"

"Yes, he does." Reggie smiled at the happiness on her son's face. "Now go wash your hands. Then you can come back and finish your breakfast. We have to leave in ten minutes."

Tad scampered down the hall and was back in less than a minute, his hands dripping.

"Are you taking Tad to town?" Angus asked.

"Yes. I drop him at school and take care of anything I need to do in town before I head back."

"I'd like to go with you," Angus said.

Reggie shot a quick glance at CW, her pulse picking up. Driving to town with Angus wouldn't be a problem on the way in. Tad would be with them, giving her something to focus on rather than the big ranch hand she'd kissed the night before. The way back, alone with the cowboy, would be an entirely different matter.

CW nodded. "Anything I have for Angus can wait until he gets back. Could use another bag or two of grain for the cattle and a bucket of fence staples from the hardware store. I forgot to pick some up yesterday."

"I can do all that without Angus's help. Isn't he needed more out here than in town?" Reggie insisted.

"No," CW said. "Like I said, what I have for him can wait. In fact I need those staples for the fence I want him to mend."

"I can lift a bucket of fence staples," Reggie said.

Jo clucked her tongue. "Ms. Reggie, let the man go with you. He needs to know where things are in town. The sooner you show him around, the less he has to bother you next time he makes a run for supplies."

Outnumbered, Reggie sighed. "Okay. We leave in five minutes."

Five minutes later Reggie walked out the front door, looking for Tad. In the driveway, Angus stood beside a big, four-wheel-drive, shiny black pickup, holding the door. Angus had removed the booster seat from her truck and installed it in his own. Tad waved from the backseat, securely buckled in.

Reggie frowned. She'd intended to take her truck into town and didn't like it when someone changed her plans without informing her first.

She stared at the truck without climbing in. "Big, fancy truck for a ranch hand."

He shrugged. "I got a deal I couldn't refuse. Are you ready?"

"I'd rather go in my ranch truck. I'd be afraid I'd scratch this one."

"And disappoint your son?" He shot a glance at the boy who was grinning from ear to ear. "Tad thought it was a great adventure to get to ride in the monster truck. I didn't have the heart to tell him it wasn't a monster truck."

Her frown lightening, she let go of her misgivings. "Okay, then. I guess we'll go in your truck."

Angus stood beside the door and held out a hand.

She ignored it and climbed up into the truck.

Before she could change her mind, he closed the door behind her.

"Mamma, I get to ride in the monster truck."

"Yes, sweetie, you do. Please remember to thank Angus for the ride."

Angus slid in behind the wheel and started the truck. With his left foot, he pressed the brake, shifted into Drive and then hit the accelerator, again with his left foot, his right foot tucked behind it.

Reggie made a note of it. Most people drove using their right foot to power the gas pedal and the break. Not wanting to make a big deal of it in front of Tad, she clamped her lips shut and saved that inquiry for later when she had Angus alone.

They made the trip into Fool's Fortune with

Tad asking Angus one question after another, from why were there so many bumps on the big tires, to what made birds sing and when would the next volcano erupt.

Each question, Angus answered with patience and intelligence, treating Tad like an adult with a mind and a need to know, yet gearing his answer in terms the child would understand.

As they slid to a stop in the drop-off line at the school, Tad said, "Thank you for bringing me to school in your monster truck. Will you pick me up, too?"

"I don't know," Reggie said. "He has to work on fences today. He might be out on the ranch too far to come get you."

Tad's face sank.

"I can drive you to school next time we need things from the feed and hardware stores."

The boy's face brightened and he unbuckled his seat belt—so grown up. "Thanks." Tad leaned over the back of the seat and hugged Reggie then surprised Angus with a hug, as well.

"I'll get the door," Reggie said and started to climb out.

"I can do it by myself." Tad opened the door and scrambled down from the big truck. He stood with his backpack on the curb and slammed the door.

Her baby was growing up. Reggie's eyes stung

as she waved, along with Angus. Tad turned and hurried into the school.

Angus shifted into Drive. "That's a great kid you've got there."

Reggie laughed, her voice a bit choked. "Yeah, he is."

"Must have been really hard to lose your husband. A boy like that needs a father."

Reggie glanced back the direction Tad had gone. "He's got me. I'm both mother and father to him right now."

"It's a big job."

"Worth every heartache," she whispered.

"Agreed." Angus's lips twisted. "My father raised me. He was both mom and dad to me after my mother died. Sure had his hands full. He even learned how to sew to put patches on my Boy Scout uniform."

"Sounds like a good man." While he drove, she could study him without fear of being caught.

"He is."

"Where is he now?"

"He retired as foreman to a large ranch and bought a little piece of land in northeast Texas. Dad remarried. Now he and his wife farm blueberries for the local markets."

"Sounds like he's found a life for himself after losing a loved one."

"It took him a while to let go. He and my

mother married straight out of high school. He took it hard when she died of cancer."

Reggie sat in silence, understanding completely what Angus's father had gone through. His story was so much like hers it almost brought tears to her eyes for the man's loss. "How long did it take your father to remarry?"

"Ten years. He said he had to find a woman who could put up with him and all his bad habits."

Reggie stared out the window. Ten years. Would it be that long before she let herself fall in love with someone again? Did she want to wait that long?

In her peripheral vision, she watched Angus maneuver the truck through the streets of the little town.

What would it be like to be in love with a man like Angus? A stranger? After marrying her first love and best friend...it would be different. Risky.

Perhaps she secretly craved something so different from what she'd had with Ted, afraid she'd confuse the two otherwise. How awful would it be if she called Angus "Ted"? Wait, she already had when he'd found her in the barn. For a brief moment when his face had been hidden in the shadows, she hadn't recognized him.

What would Ted think of Angus? Would he approve of her daring to start over with another man? She wished she could talk with Ted, ask his permission to start dating.

Not that she wanted to.

A year certainly wasn't ten years. And Angus was the hired hand, not date material. Though that kiss...

"I take it this is the only hardware store in town."

While she'd been lost in her thoughts about Ted and Angus, the ranch hand had pulled up in front of Fortune Hardware. "This is it, and we're lucky to have it. Too many small towns have closed their hardware stores and residents have to travel to one of the larger towns or into Denver for supplies."

"I grew up in a small town. The owner of the hardware store held on by a thread for years. Finally the feed store owner bought him out and combined inventory to provide for the local ranchers."

"Some people would feel stranded living out in the hills like we do here in Fool's Fortune."

"I can't imagine that. It's a beautiful place." He stared out across the mountains.

"This town was founded by miners back in the gold rush era. Its population has shrunk since I was a little girl. I suspect the high school would have closed long ago if they hadn't absorbed the schools from the neighboring towns. I'd hate to see Fool's Fortune become a ghost town like so many others. If not for the ranching and tourism, we wouldn't have as much as we do."

Angus shifted into Park. "Are you coming in?"

"No. I need to drop into the bank. Tell the hardware store owner that you're working for me and to put whatever you need on my account."

Reggie didn't wait for Angus to get out and come around to open her door. She slid out of her seat and dropped to the ground before he had a chance to get out himself.

Angus met her in front of the truck. "You'll be okay?"

Reggie frowned. "Why wouldn't I be?"

He nodded toward the lump on her forehead. She'd left her hair hanging loose and some of it angled down, hiding the knot and bruising. "Whoever hit you is probably here in town."

"You think so?" Her pulse quickened and her gaze darted around.

"I meant to tell you last night that I found a two-by-four with blood on it."

"And you waited until now to tell me?"

"I got...distracted before I could tell you last night when I came in."

Her face grew red and she glanced away. "Could have been one from a fence a cow had run into."

Angus shook his head. "There were also fresh tire tracks beside the board, from what appeared to be a four-wheeler, and footprints near the back of the barn that didn't belong to CW or me." He touched her arm. "I'm concerned and I believe you should be, too."

"Why are you concerned?" She tilted her head. "You barely know me." Surely their kiss hadn't meant more to him than she suspected.

He gave her a half grin. "You're the boss. If something happens to you, I'll be out of a job."

For a moment her stomach sank. What did she expect? The man was more concerned about his job than her. She squared her shoulders. Last night's kiss obviously hadn't inspired him as much as it had her.

Promising herself to steer clear of kissing this man, Reggie hurried toward the bank. Somehow, no matter how far apart they were, she still couldn't get him off her mind.

ANGUS ENTERED THE hardware store, knowing there were three prime places in a small town to find information. The hardware store, the feed store and the main diner. Men were prone to gossip as much, if not more, than women. At least that was what he was banking on.

He went straight for the counter and found an older man he hoped was the owner or a long-time employee.

The man nodded politely. "Can I help you?"

Angus stuck out his hand. "I'm Angus Ketchum, the new ranch hand at the Last Chance Ranch."

"Raymond Cramer, owner of this establishment." The older man took his hand and gave it a firm shake. "Didn't know Ms. Reggie and CW were hirin'." He let go and brushed his hand across his jeans. "You're not from around these parts." It was a statement, not a question.

"No, sir."

"You're not one of those city boys who doesn't know the business end of a horse, are ya?"

Angus chuckled. "No, sir." The hard part about an outsider coming in and asking questions of the locals was gaining their trust. "I'm from Texas. I grew up on a cattle ranch. I've been ridin' and working with cattle since I was old enough to sit a saddle."

The older man's eyes narrowed as if he was sizing him up. Finally he said. "Don't know why they didn't hire local, but if ya got experience, can't blame 'em. What can I do ya for?"

"We could use ten pounds of fence staples."

"Got those right over here." Raymond Cramer led him down an aisle with old-fashioned wooden bins filled with nails and screws of all shapes and sizes. He stopped at the end, where clear plastic buckets were stacked containing different sizes of fence staples.

Angus selected what he needed and hefted the bucket.

"Anything else you need?" Cramer asked.

"Nothing yet. I'm sure I'll be back when I've

had a chance to give the place a good lookin' around." He followed Cramer back to the counter, where the man wrote out a paper receipt and rang up his purchase on a cash register older than Angus.

"How's Ms. Reggie holdin' up without Ted to help out?" Cramer asked, showing him the total.

Angus took out his wallet and selected several bills and laid them on the counter. He didn't feel right, putting such a small amount on the ranch account. "She's got her hands full."

"Ain't right. That poor woman shouldn't have to manage that ranch with only CW there to help. Not that she isn't capable. It's just not right, livin' out that far. She should sell while the market's hot."

"What's hot about the market for ranch land in the foothills?"

Cramer handed him his change. "That's right. You're new around here. There've been speculators out buying up land. They claim that with their new-fangled mining equipment, they can extract gold and silver they never thought they could get to before."

Angus lifted the bucket of staples from the counter. "I understand these hills were ripe with prospectors back in the gold rush."

"That's right. Never found much around here—not for lack of trying. Thus the name of the town, Fool's Fortune. Only mine worth much was the Lucky Lady Mine, and that played out in the early nineteen hundreds." Cramer leaned his elbow against the high counter. "My great-grandfather mined those hills and never found more than an ounce of gold. He got smart and established this hardware store in the eighteen seventies. That's where he made his fortune. Sellin' supplies to the prospectors. Bunch of fools."

"Are the speculators still in town?" Angus asked.

"They were holed up at the Gold Rush Tavern last I heard. They've been busy, out trying to buy up the land around these parts. Between them and the yuppies from California and Denver, a body can't afford to live around here much anymore."

"Had to deal with oil speculators back in Texas. Some of them could be pretty pushy."

"You got that right. They prey on the older people and those folks who are tired of eking out a living on the land. And don't get me started on Daniel Freeman and his ragged group of survivalists. They'll squat anywhere they think they can get away with it and then fight to protect it as if it was theirs to begin with. Good Lord. Colorado ain't what it used to be. And I can't say it makes me happy."

"Times are changing," Angus agreed. "I remember riding for miles across open prairie with nothing but grass and cattle. Now those same prairies are dotted with oilrigs and pumps. Not nearly as pretty."

Cramer shook his head. "I hate to think what this place would look like if they came in and did some of that open-pit mining. Might have to sell out and move to Florida so I don't have to be here when it happens."

"Mr. Cramer—"

"Call me Raymond. 'Mr.' makes me feel old."

"Yes, sir." Angus smiled.

"You must have spent some time in the military."

"I did." His smile slipped. He'd still be in the military if he hadn't been crippled.

Raymond Cramer nodded. "Ain't often you get young folks with manners anymore."

"Do you know Ms. Davis well?" Angus asked, risking alienating the man by asking too much too soon.

"Knew her parents. Watched her grow up and marry young Ted Davis. She's a good woman."

"Is there anyone who'd want to hurt her or the Last Chance Ranch?"

Raymond leaned forward, his bushy gray brows running together. "CW mentioned there'd been a few accidents around the place lately. Was Ms. Reggie hurt?"

Angus didn't want to alarm the man, but he wanted to know what to expect. "She would say they were accidents but, as an outsider looking in, I have my doubts."

Cramer straightened. "That girl never hurt a fly. She helps out when folks need help and she's always been nice to everyone. No one would want to hurt her that I know of.

"As for the ranch, it's been in the Davis family for nearly a century. The land is too rugged and hilly to do much ranching, but they've managed to keep cattle and make a living off it." He stared across the counter at Angus. "Sure would hate to see anything bad happen to Ms. Reggie. You keep an eye on her, will ya? And that boy of hers. What with no daddy to look out for him, he's already at a disadvantage."

"I'll do the best I can," Angus promised. He lifted the bucket of staples. "Thank you for your help, Mr. Cr—Raymond." He smiled. "It's a pleasure to do business with you."

"Same to you. And thank you for your service to this great country."

Angus left the store, processing the information he'd gleaned from the owner. He felt a connection with Mr. Cramer and the town called Fool's Fortune. He could also see where the town and the landowners surrounding it could be at risk of greedy mining companies.

Reggie had her hands full just managing a ranch and her son's life. She sure didn't need the added pressure of speculators or survivalists breathing down her back—or hitting her in the head with two-by-fours.

Accidents? *No way.*

Chapter Six

Reggie left the bank discouraged. Her account was nearing empty and she still hadn't gotten the cattle down from the upper pastures and loaded up for auction.

Though she received a monthly check from Ted's life insurance annuity, it was never enough to pay for everything, and now she had another ranch hand to pay. Cattle prices being what they were, the few steers she had to sell wouldn't cover ranch hand pay for long. If they had a harsh winter, she might run out of hay for the remaining cattle and end up selling them at a loss or investing more in hay to feed them through the winter.

No matter how she looked at it, she'd just have to let Angus go. Tad would be disappointed. Her son had established an immediate attachment to the man that bordered on hero worship. And Angus had promised to teach him how to ride.

If she admitted it to herself, he'd made an

equal impression on her. A man with a problem leg, he'd rescued her from being trampled, no matter what she'd told him to the contrary, and twice had picked her up and carried her as if she weighed nothing at all. And though his arms were strong, she suspected he'd suffered pain in his legs, but he'd never said a word and never complained.

Out in the cool December sunshine, she spied Angus settling a bucket in the bed of his pickup. She might as well break the news to him right away. He'd need time to look for another job.

With that in mind, she marched down the sidewalk toward him.

"Reggie Davis. Long time no see," a woman's voice called out.

Reggie turned toward the doorway of the local diner. Kitty Toland stood in the open door, wiping her hands on an apron. "Please tell me you were coming by to say hello."

Guilt assailed Reggie at the sight of her oldest and dearest friend from high school. "Kitty." She glanced at Angus briefly and headed for the diner to hug her friend. "Get inside before you catch your death, woman."

"I'm fine. I've been helping out in the kitchen, and you know how hot it gets in there."

"I thought you hired a cook."

"I did, but I'm still in the process of training her on all the items on the menu." She pulled

Reggie through the door and wrapped her in her arms. "How's my best friend?"

"Fine. Just very busy."

Kitty held her at arm's length. "You look tired. Are you working too hard on that ranch? Woman, how many times do I have to tell you it's too much for just one person?"

"It's not just me. I have CW."

"He's getting too old to help out much. Which leaves all the heavy work for you." Kitty shook her head and hugged her again. "You need to sell that place and move to the city. You work too hard."

Reggie laughed. "Says the woman who owns the most successful diner in all of Fool's Fortune. You must put eighty hours a week in this place."

She shrugged. "What else do I have to do? There are no men to date in this town."

"Exactly." Her mind shifted to the ranch hand she had been about to fire. "Why don't you sell and move to Denver? I'm sure you could land a job as a cook in one of those fancy restaurants. You have the training and the experience and you're wasting it on this little Podunk town."

"It's my home. I can't imagine living anywhere else."

"Lady, you've been to Paris." Reggie shook her head. "There are plenty of other places to live than Fool's Fortune."

Kitty smiled. "They don't call it Fool's Fortune

for nothing. I'm just one more fool claiming it as home. I like your hair down, you should wear it that way more often." She pushed aside the strand of hair Reggie had let fall over the bruise on her forehead.

Bracing herself, Reggie waited for her friend's surprise.

Kitty's eyes widened. "What the hell, Reggie? How did you get this?"

Reggie captured her wrist and pulled her hand away from her face. "I bumped my head."

"No way. I'd heard rumor things were kind of weird out at the ranch—that there had been several accidents. Honey, that doesn't look like an accident to me." She glanced over her shoulder. "The sheriff was here just a moment ago. Where'd he go?"

"I don't want to talk to the sheriff. For all I know, it could have been an accident. I was working in the barn…the lights went out…something could have fallen on me." Even as she said the words, she knew they weren't true. Someone had deliberately hit her.

"The lights went out? And who might have turned them out?"

"You know that barn is older than dirt. No telling how long it's been since the electrical wires have been updated. A big wind could have knocked it out."

"Last night was the first night in a week the

winds were calm. I know. I was outside empty-ing the trash after dark. I didn't have to fight the lid on the trash bin to get it opened or closed."

"I don't know exactly how the lights went out." Reggie sighed. "Can you leave it?"

"I still think you should march yourself down to the sheriff's office and report what's happened so far. At least they could keep an eye out for someone acting suspiciously."

"If it makes you feel better, I will."

"Damn right you will." Kitty crossed her arms over her chest as the bell over the front door rang, announcing a customer's arrival. "Oh, my. Per-haps I spoke too soon about nobody to date in this Podunk town." She hooked her arm through Reggie's. "Look what just walked through the door, all tall, dark and sexy."

Reggie frowned and turned with Kitty to face the newcomer. Her heart fluttered and skipped several beats as Angus ducked through the door and smiled at her.

"There you are," Angus said. "I got the staples and the feed."

Kitty's eyebrows rose into her hairline. "You know this hunkilicious man?" she whispered.

With a sigh, Reggie had to admit the man could stir her blood all too easily. "Kitty, this is Angus Ketchum, my new ranch hand. Angus, this is my old friend Kitty Toland."

Kitty frowned playfully. "Not so old, but, yes,

longtime friend. Hello, cowboy. It's very nice to meet you." Kitty held out her hand, batting her eyelids like a silly schoolgirl.

Though she loved her friend, Reggie didn't like the hungry gleam in Kitty's eyes when she feasted her gaze on Angus.

Not that Reggie had any claim to the man other than that he worked for her at the ranch. And she'd been about to end that employment when Kitty had pulled her aside.

Angus took her hand and gave it a firm shake. "Pleasure's mine." He held on to Kitty's hand long enough to make Reggie's back teeth grind before he let go and turned his attention to Reggie. "I'd like to drop by the tavern for a moment before we leave town, if you have the time."

"If you're hungry," Kitty said, "the food is better here at the diner."

Reggie smiled. "She's not being boastful, it's true. You can get anything from hamburgers to French cuisine. Kitty's a trained chef."

"I'm not hungry. I wanted to stop to see if someone is staying there."

"That should work out great." Kitty gave Reggie a smug look. "Make sure Reggie stops at the sheriff's office. It's on the way."

"I have cattle to bring down from a high pasture, I can't spend the whole day in town," Reggie argued.

Kitty touched Angus's arm. "She needs to

report that nasty bump on her head. I want to have her around when I grow old so I can tease her about going gray." She winked at Angus.

Reggie's lips thinned. "Fine. But let's not make a big deal of it. It was an accident."

Angus leaned close to Kitty. "It wasn't."

Kitty snorted. "I figured as much."

"Have there been any other incidents reported in or around Fool's Fortune?" Angus asked.

"Nothing but the goings-on out at the Last Chance Ranch," Kitty said.

"Have there been any strangers hanging around town?"

Kitty touched a finger to her chin and stared off into a corner. "There are the usual retirees who come to shop for antiques and the occasional biker passing through. But I don't know of anyone actually hanging around. Except maybe the mining speculators."

"Mining speculators?" Angus pinned her with his gaze. "What about them?"

Reggie waved a hand. "They've been hanging around trying to buy up land in the area. They've been out several times to the ranch, and I keep telling them I'm not interested in selling."

"Could they be trying to scare you off your ranch?" Kitty asked.

Reggie shrugged. "I doubt it. They seemed nice enough."

Angus focused on Kitty. "Will you let me know if anyone looks or acts suspicious?"

"You bet," Kitty responded.

Reggie shook her head. "Now you're both being paranoid."

Kitty patted her arm. "We love ya, sweetie." To Angus she said, "Take care of my girl, will ya?"

"Yes, ma'am." Angus saluted her.

Reggie rolled her eyes. "I don't need someone to take care of me."

"You're so busy taking care of everyone else, someone needs to take care of you, honey." Kitty hugged her. "Don't be such a stranger."

"The road goes both ways," Reggie reminded her.

"I know, I know. I'm going to take an evening off as soon as I feel comfortable my cook and wait staff can handle it without me."

"Sweetie, you need to get a life," Reggie said.

"Ditto." Kitty walked them to the door and opened it, setting the bell above to ringing. A gust of cool mountain air blew through. "Brrr. It won't be long before we get snow. Promise me you won't be out pushing cows around the hills."

"Herding cows." Reggie smiled. "If I don't get out of here, I will be herding cattle in the snow."

Kitty waved goodbye and quickly released the door, rubbing her arms as she turned back into the diner.

Reggie stared a moment longer through the window at Kitty. "I need to get to town more often."

"She seems like a good friend."

"The best. And I don't visit enough. Seems like I'm always too busy." Since Ted died, she had barely had time to run into town, grab feed and groceries and head back. Never mind getting a haircut or seeing the friend she'd grown up with. When had her life become so intense?

"Which way?" Angus held the door for her.

Reggie climbed into the truck. "To get to the tavern, take a left at the only light in town. We really don't have to stop at the sheriff's office. I only told Kitty I would to make her happy."

Angus climbed into the driver's side. A minute later they pulled into the parking lot of the sheriff's office. "We're stopping," he said as he shifted into Park.

"This really isn't necessary. The sheriff doesn't believe I should be running that ranch on my own, anyway. He'll think it's all female hysterics."

"Then we'll speak to a deputy. The sooner we document the incidents, the sooner someone keeps an eye out for trouble."

Reggie didn't make a move to get out of the truck.

"Is the sheriff that bad?" Angus asked.

"No. I just don't want anyone thinking I'm not

capable of taking care of the Last Chance Ranch on my own." And, yes, the sheriff was that much of an egotistical jerk.

"Put it this way," Angus started, "what if you're not the only one on the receiving end of attacks like this? How will the local law enforcement establish a pattern if you don't report it? You could be prolonging a bigger issue than just what's happening on the ranch."

Reggie unbuckled her seat belt. "God, I hate it that you make sense." She climbed out of the truck and walked with him into the sheriff's office. Thankfully, a deputy was on duty. The sheriff was nowhere around. Reggie gave her statement, listing out the incidents. She ended with, "I don't know if they were truly accidents, but if it's happening to anyone else, I didn't want to hold back information that might lead to finding who is responsible."

"Reggie Davis." A voice boomed behind her and made her flinch.

She turned slowly, her back stiffening as her chin rose. "Good morning, Sheriff."

The man stuck out his hand to Angus. "I don't believe I've had the pleasure."

Angus shook the man's hand. "Angus Ketchum."

"I didn't realize Reggie had a new man in her life."

"I don't," Reggie stated flatly. Not that it was

any of his business. "He's my new ranch hand. Angus, Sheriff Harris."

"What brings you by the office?" Sheriff Harris glanced over Reggie's shoulder to the deputy beyond.

"Ms. Davis was reporting several incidents," the deputy said.

The sheriff stared hard at Reggie. "Everything all right out there?" He shook his head. "Told you it was begging for trouble, you living out there by yourself."

"I don't live by myself. The Reinhardts live right next to me and Tad." She tilted her head toward Angus. "And now Angus."

The sheriff nodded. "Not much help for such a large spread and being so far out."

She grit her teeth to keep from telling the sheriff to mind his own business and that she wasn't completely inept. "We manage just fine."

"Not if you're reporting problems. When are you going to give it up and sell?"

Heat rose in her neck and all the way up to the top of her head. Though she knew better than to antagonize the sheriff, she couldn't stop herself from saying, "When are you going to quit asking?" She hooked Angus's arm. "Excuse us. We have work to do."

Practically dragging the man to the door, she almost made it through on the last word.

"That place is too much for a lone woman. And this report proves it."

When Angus stopped, Reggie kept going, dragging him along. "Don't listen to him, he's a chauvinistic pig. Comes from a long line of them."

"He had no right to belittle you for running a ranch by yourself. A woman is every bit as capable as a man."

"Not in Sheriff Harris's opinion. If he had his way, I'd sell to some man so that he wouldn't feel like he might actually have to drive that far out to investigate a crime. As if a man wouldn't have the same difficulties I've experienced."

Angus took her hand and squeezed it. "I was impressed you didn't say any more than you did."

"It was bad enough I said what I did. It only riles the man and makes him want to prove a point with me. Well, to hell with him. I'm running a ranch. It's my son's heritage. I'll preserve it for him if I have to go to work waiting tables at the diner to make enough money to live there."

"Are finances that bad?"

Reggie could have bitten her tongue. "As a matter of fact, I wanted to talk to you about—"

"I told you, how much you pay me isn't that important."

"Thing is, I can't pay you. I barely have enough in my bank account to pay CW. I don't know why he didn't clear hiring you with me before he did it." She took in a deep breath and let it out slowly. "I'm afraid I have to let you go."

Chapter Seven

Angus almost chuckled at the woman's concern. He didn't know how much he could share about his position on the ranch, and that he didn't need to be paid at all. Hank was paying him for this job.

He respected Reggie enough to want to be honest with her, but he didn't want anyone else to know he'd been hired to protect her. CW had made him promise not to let on that he'd been hired as more of a bodyguard than a ranch hand.

"Don't worry about it." Angus settled behind the wheel of the pickup. Now that he'd met Reggie and witnessed her fierce independence, he knew exactly what her reaction would be if she learned he was there to provide protection. She'd get her hackles up and demand he leave.

Then she'd be out on the ranch with only an old man, an old woman and a small child. No, to stick around and make sure nothing bad happened to her, he had to continue with the charade.

"I don't need pay. All I need is room and board."

"You have to have some bills. How will you pay for this big ol' truck?"

"I'm retired from the military," he said. "I get a pension. I don't need the money. I just need to work."

"But you could work somewhere that would pay you."

"I like it at the Last Chance Ranch. And Ranger does, too."

"But—"

"Look, give me a month. I'm sure you can use some help and I need to stay busy. Retirement isn't my style."

She frowned. "You're not old enough to be retired from the military."

"I'm older than you think." At least physically and mentally he was older, if not in actual years. On days the pain took its toll, he felt a hundred.

Her eyes narrowed. "How old are you?"

"That's information you don't need to know."

"Aha! You're holding out on me. If there's one thing I can't tolerate, it's being lied to."

"I'll do my best not to lie to you." Technically, omission of the truth wasn't a lie. A stab of guilt ripped through him but he quickly pushed it aside. If omitting the truth was the only way to get Reggie to let him stay, so be it. He wasn't there to win her love. He was there to keep her alive.

It would take a lot more to win this woman's heart. A whole man, who wasn't riddled with the nightmares brought on by PTSD, and a lot more time than he'd be at her ranch. He shifted into Reverse and pulled out of the parking lot faster than he intended, surprised at the anger and frustration he thought he'd conquered. The months of rehabilitation had prepared him for life without the use of one leg, but nothing could compare to living among able-bodied men and women who'd never dealt with the kind of injury he and other military men and women had sustained.

The rehab center had been filled with people just like him. It was easy to rally around each other and provide encouragement. Now that he was out on his own, he didn't have that support system. And he didn't need it. He could do almost anything other men with two legs could do.

"The tavern is two blocks down and across the street." Reggie pointed to a two-story building sporting an old-fashioned false storefront, a balcony overlooking the street and wide porches on the ground level with benches for passersby. On a sign across the top painted in large gold lettering were the words Gold Rush Tavern & Hotel.

Reggie's lips quirked upward. "The owners refurbished it and gave it a look they hoped would appeal to the tourists."

"Does it?"

She nodded. "It does. That, the trick pony

show and the mock gunfights in the streets during the summer brings in a lot of tourist dollars. Why did you want to come here?"

"I wanted to talk to the speculators who are in town trying to buy up land around here."

Reggie's frown deepened. "You think they might be the ones who are causing the problems out at the ranch?"

"Could be." He glanced across at her as he pulled into a parking space in front of the tavern. "Are you coming in?"

"Hell, yeah." She pushed the door open and climbed out.

They entered the tavern together and walked up to the hotel reception desk.

"May I help you?" a pretty young woman asked.

Reggie stepped forward. "Briana Jordan?"

When Reggie smiled at the young woman, it nearly bowled Angus over. It was bright, friendly and made his heart beat faster. That he noticed it so much was proof she didn't smile nearly often enough. He found himself wanting to make her do it again.

The young woman blinked and nodded. "Yes, ma'am?"

Reggie's smile broadened. "The last time I saw you, you were fourteen with braces."

Her cheeks pinkened and her chin tilted upward. "I turned eighteen three months ago. I'm working through the holidays to save money for tuition. I'm starting college next fall."

"Congratulations. Tell your mother and father Reggie Davis said hello."

"I'll do that." She smiled. "Now, how can I help you?"

"I'm interested in speaking with the mining speculators who are here in town. I believe one of them is Vance Peterson."

Briana ducked her head and tapped the keyboard of a computer for a full minute before she looked up. "He's the only one left in town. The others have gone home for the Christmas holidays. Want me to ring Mr. Peterson's room?"

"Please." Reggie backed away from the desk and waited.

Briana lifted a phone to her ear and tapped keys on the base unit. After a few moments she returned the receiver to its cradle. "I'm sorry, but there was no answer. Could I leave a message?"

"No, thank you," Reggie said. "We'll try to catch him later."

"He might be over at the county courthouse. He spends a lot of time looking up land plats. Either there or at the Fool's Fortune real estate office."

"Thanks again, Briana. And congratulations on college." Reggie headed for the door.

Angus beat her there and opened it for her.

"I can open my own door," she muttered.

His mouth twitched at the sides, but he forced back his grin. "Sometimes I think you try too hard to be self-sufficient and independent."

"When it comes right down to it, the only one you can count on is yourself," she said. "If you don't do what has to be done, it might never get done."

"What happened to trust?"

"It's not so much a matter of trust. It's practical. If there isn't anyone else around to do it, I have to do it myself." She straightened her back. "If I don't know how, I damn well better learn."

"You can hire help to handle things you can't do yourself."

"I can't afford to." She tipped her chin up. "Besides, I haven't found too many things I can't do."

"I'd believe that." Angus stopped at the passenger door to his pickup and opened it for her.

She paused with her foot on the running board and stared up at him. "You think that makes me less feminine, don't you?"

"Not at all." He grinned. "I think it makes you sexy as hell."

Angus was almost as surprised he'd voiced his thoughts as Reggie probably was to hear them.

The only sign his words affected her was the soft rose shading climbing up her cheeks and the brief flare of her eyes. If he wasn't mistaken, she'd liked his compliment.

And it made him want to pull her into his arms and show her how much he meant it.

Before he could reach out and do just that, she snorted softly. "Sexy, my fanny." She climbed up into the truck and sat, her face redder than before.

"That, too." He winked at her. "The 'sexy fanny' part." Before she could retort, he shut the door and whistled on his way around the truck.

As he stepped up onto the running board with his prosthetic leg, pain shot up his thigh and he staggered backward. If he hadn't been holding on to the door, he'd have fallen flat on his butt.

"Angus?" Reggie leaned across the seat. "Are you okay?"

"I'm fine," he muttered. Angry that he'd let himself relax enough to think he could be any other guy flirting with a pretty woman, he turned to hide the pain from her concerned gaze. The last thing he needed was her sympathy. Hell, he was there to help her, not become yet another burden for her to manage.

The click of a door opening on the other side made him straighten. "I said I'm fine," he said through tight lips.

"Like hell you are." Before he could protest, Reggie stood beside him, her blue eyes dark. "Did you hurt yourself?" She bent to touch his leg.

He jerked backward. "I don't need your help. Get in the damn truck."

Reggie flinched, retracting her hand. When she straightened, her eyes flashed. "I'll get in the damn truck when I'm good and damn ready. Now tell me what's wrong, or do I have to figure it out on my own as if you were a baby too small to voice where his booboos are?" She planted her fists on her hips and her long, sandy-blond hair whipped back in a sudden gust of wind.

God, she was beautiful. And so far out of his reach his hands ached to hold her. For a long moment he clenched his fists, wanting to rage at the injustice. Then he reminded himself of how lucky he actually was. All the time he'd spent in physical therapy, he'd worked alongside paraplegics learning how to get around in wheel-chairs. Or soldiers who'd lost both legs, adjusting to their new lives. Slowly he unclenched his fists. "I'm sorry. I shouldn't have snapped at you."

"Apology accepted. Now tell me what just happened."

"Nothing. Just a war injury flaring up."

"Your right leg?" She nodded toward the jeans-clad prosthetic.

Still unwilling to reveal everything, he nod-ded. Let her believe what she wanted. "Yes, ma'am. The doctors call it phantom pain."

She shook her head. "And you carried me all the way to the house from the barn in pain, didn't you?"

That look of sympathy hit him in the gut.

"Look, it's something I can live with. And I don't need your or anyone else's sympathy. And if you're worried whether or not I can do the work, don't. I can do anything you can and more."

The soft look in her eyes hardened. "Well, then, let's get to it. We've wasted enough time in town. I have cattle in an upper pasture that need to be brought down before the snow or they'll die." She marched around to the other side of the truck and climbed in. "Well?"

His anger, along with the pain, sliding away, Angus got in and drove through town and out the other side. They completed the drive in silence all the way up to the house. When he shifted into Park, Reggie laid a hand on his arm.

"One of these days, I hope that you can speak freely of your time in the service and your injury. For now, I'll accept that you don't want to. Like you said, sometimes you have to trust someone else."

She didn't wait for his response, climbing down from the truck.

Angus's chest tightened along with his grip on the steering wheel.

Reggie turned back. "Come on, cowboy. We have work to do."

His heart lightening, he got out, threw the sack of feed over his shoulder, grabbed the bucket of fence staples and followed her to the barn.

She'd already led her horse out of his stall, tied him to a post and then headed for the tack room.

CW took the bucket of staples out of his hands. "I'll work the fence. Ms. Reggie needs help getting the cattle down to the lower pasture. The weatherman is predicting snow in the next thirty-six hours." CW jerked his head toward the stall behind him. "You can take Red. He has about the best manners of any horse we've got on this place."

Swallowing his pride, Angus thanked CW. An expert rider before the war, he didn't know how he'd fare with one good leg. Thankful for the chance to ride on a horse that knew what he was doing, he didn't argue for a more spirited one. Instead he followed Reggie into the tack room. She was lifting a saddle off a saddletree when he came up behind her. As she started to turn, she bumped into him.

His arms went around her and he grabbed the saddle.

With her back pressed against his front, he didn't want to move and couldn't think past how good she felt and how her hair smelled like honeysuckle.

For a second they were suspended in the moment.

A throat cleared behind Angus, breaking the spell.

"Sorry," Angus said. "I didn't mean to bump

into you. You have it?" He didn't let go until he was certain she wasn't going to drop it.

Reggie nodded.

Angus stepped away and grabbed a blanket, bridle and a saddle from the row of saddletrees on the wall. When he turned, Reggie was gone.

CW was there, his eyes narrowed. "Ms. Reggie is special."

"I know."

"She's been through enough with Mr. Davis's death."

"I understand."

"Don't break her heart." CW stood in the doorway a moment longer. "That's all I've got to say." The older man turned and walked away.

Angus stood still for a moment longer, digesting CW's warning. The old man obviously had him confused with someone who could capture Reggie's heart. The woman loved her dead husband. She wasn't over her grief.

The kiss she'd shared with him might indicate she was starting to think along those lines. But not with him. He was just a ranch hand.

A ranch hand that needed to get moving and help the owner drive her cattle out of the hills. He pushed thoughts of their kiss to the back of his mind, fully aware of CW's warning.

Reggie had the saddle on her horse and was cinching the girth when Angus emerged from the tack room.

She glanced up at him. "Better hurry or we won't have enough time to get up there and back before dark. I'll stop by the house for something for lunch. You'll need gloves, and is that your warmest jacket?"

CW had led Red out of the stall and tied him next to Reggie's gelding.

Angus tossed the saddle blanket over the horse's back and the saddle on top of it. He had the girth cinched by the time Reggie had slipped the bridle over her mount's face.

"Yes, ma'am. This is my warmest jacket." Angus slipped a bridle over Red's head.

Reggie studied him for a moment. "You might be used to cattle ranching in Texas, but in the Colorado Rockies, the temperatures can plummet sixty degrees in hours. I suggest, while I'm packing lunch, you slip on a thermal undershirt or a sweatshirt beneath your jacket. If we get caught out overnight, I don't want you freezing to death."

He didn't remind her that nights in a West Texas wintertime could get as cold as the mountains. Instead he gave her a mock salute. "Yes, ma'am."

Reggie walked her gelding through the barn door.

Angus tightened the straps on Red's bridle.

CW handed him a pair of gloves as he moved

past him. He didn't say a word, but his expression said it all. *Take care of our girl.*

Walking his horse up to the house, Angus tied it to a convenient hitching post near the porch and entered the house through the kitchen.

Reggie stood at the counter in her boots, jeans and outdoor jacket, wrapping sandwiches in cellophane and stuffing them into a saddlebag. She'd pulled her hair back into a ponytail, making her appear as young as a teenager, her face fresh and clean.

Hunger of a different kind filled Angus and he hurried through the room and down the hallway. He shrugged out of his jacket, slipped an old Army sweatshirt over his head and pulled it down over his chambray shirt. He pulled his leg up and checked his prosthetic, adjusting it to fit perfectly. If it was off just a little, it would disturb the calluses he'd built up since he'd first learned to walk with it. The boot he'd fitted over the end was snug and wouldn't fall off easily.

"Angus, are you ready to go?" Reggie's voice sounded behind him.

He yanked the pant leg down over his prosthetic and straightened. "Will this do?" He held out his arms, hoping to distract her from what he'd been doing.

She eyed his sweatshirt and nodded. "That, plus your jacket will help. Do you have a wool scarf?"

He shook his head.

"I'll find one for you." She entered the room across from his. Moments later she emerged with a solid gray scarf and handed it to him.

He held out his hand and she placed the scarf in it.

But she didn't let go immediately, her hands brushing over the soft wool. "It was Ted's."

Angus pushed it back toward her. "I can't wear something that belonged to your husband."

Her lips curled on the corners. "Nonsense. It's perfectly good, and it would be a waste to throw it away just because it belonged to Ted."

Reluctantly he accepted the proffered scarf. "Are you ready?"

She nodded. "We have exactly five hours to get up there, find the cattle and bring them down before the sun sets over the hilltops."

"Then let's go."

She walked with him to the back door. "How long has it been since you've been in the saddle?"

"Fourteen years."

"Uh-huh." Her mouth curled in a natural smile. "This is going to hurt."

If only she knew. Angus held the door for her, tempted to go back in, swallow one of his super pain pills and then join her. But he'd need all of his faculties around him to navigate the hilly country. He'd ridden horses in the Palo Duro Canyon of North Texas, but never with only one good leg. He recalled the strain of standing in his stirrups and how tired he'd been after the daylong trek. And that had been when he was a teenager, in the prime of his physical life.

Today would be a test of his physical therapy sessions and his ability to endure prolonged strain on his muscles. Though it was a given, he prayed the phantom pain would hold off until he returned.

More than that, he prayed whoever was out to cause Reggie problems would ease up this once and let them perform their job without incident.

Chapter Eight

Reggie led the way up the old mining road into the hills. The last time she'd seen the dozen or more head of cattle, they'd been up around the old Last Chance Mine, the mine the ranch was named after.

The mine lay a good forty-five-minute ride up into some of the rockiest hills on the spread. Forty-five minutes for an experienced rider.

She'd been concerned when Angus saddled up. He'd struggled a bit getting his right boot into the stirrup. Once there, he sat the saddle like a pro. Tall, sexy…with a cowboy hat pulled down snugly to keep the gusts of wind from whipping it off his head. He moved with the rhythm of the horse like a natural, not fighting to stay mounted.

The man stirred her blood as it hadn't been stirred in more than a year. Hell, in longer than that. She'd loved Ted more than anything, but that love had been born out of a childhood crush on her best friend. Had he lived, she'd probably have remained perfectly content and happily married, growing old with a man she loved and who loved her.

Now that Ted was gone and Angus was here, she didn't know what she was supposed to feel. The excitement burning in her gut and the electrical charge that shot through her each time he touched her left her confused, needy and wanting more. What was wrong with her?

Was Kitty right? Did she need a man in her life? She'd been getting along just fine without one. She'd worked hard over the past year to keep things going just the way Ted had. Only she'd *helped* Ted. Ted wasn't there to help *her*. CW was getting older and she liked having him stay closer to the house to tend to the barnyard animals. Occasionally he rode out with her, but not as much lately. Having him there to make sure Tad got home from school was a big relief.

Lost in her thoughts, Reggie had barely acknowledged that the trail had widened into one of the pretty mountain meadows on the ranch. In the summertime the cattle grazed in this one and others. The grass was brown now, with the night's freezing temperatures, but the snow that had fallen a couple of weeks ago had all melted.

"I bet this is a pretty spot in the summer," Angus said, riding up beside her.

"It is." She envisioned the bright splashes of blossoming columbines and dandelions amid the brilliant green of late spring grass. Her glance slid to Angus. "How are you holding up?"

He nodded. "I'm fine."

"Don't be hesitant to ask to stop and rest. I know how sore you can get if you haven't ridden in a while."

"I'll let you know."

She doubted it. The stubborn tilt of his chin told her he'd rather shoot himself than admit any kind of weakness to her. She could admire that in a man, but at the same time, she didn't suffer fools. They'd been riding a little over thirty minutes and they still had another thirty to get to where they were going.

Pointing to the other side of the meadow where a narrow trail wound up another rocky path to the top of a ridge, she said, "Last time I saw the cattle, they were up beyond that ridge and on the other side of a narrow valley below the old gold mine. It'll be another thirty minutes before we stop." She glanced his way, pausing to give him another opportunity to ask for a break.

Angus tipped his head toward the sky. "Then we better get going. Clouds are moving in and the weatherman predicted snow as early as this afternoon."

"When you reach the top of the ridge, bear to your left. There's a wicked drop-off to the right."

"Will do."

She pressed her knees into her horse's sides.

The animal set off at a trot. Angus rode alongside her until they crossed the meadow and started up the rocky trail.

As they topped the ridge, she slowed, staring down at the vertical drop-off. Every time she passed this point her heart beat faster and she was overcome with deep, heart-wrenching sadness. It was here on a stormy day that Ted had been thrown from his horse.

"Reggie?" Angus called out behind her. "Are you okay?"

She gripped her reins and clicked her tongue. Her gelding stepped forward, passing the point where her life had changed forever.

The path led along the side of a cliff and down into a narrow valley. Glancing across the valley, she could see several steers on the opposite side, grazing on whatever grass they could find. "Do you see them?" she called over her shoulder.

"Yes, ma'am."

They still had to navigate the rocky ravine at the center of the narrow valley before they reached the other side. Reggie pushed on. Reggie knew the easiest path from years of traveling every accessible inch of the ranch. She let the horse set the pace, picking its way across the rocky terrain and over a mountain stream.

On the other side, she paused and waited for Angus to catch up. She didn't have to wait long.

He'd kept up the entire way without complaint, raising him another notch in her estimation.

"We can stop here for a few minutes to rest the horses and let them drink." She slid out of her saddle, dropped to the ground and then reached for the saddlebag.

In her peripheral vision, she observed Angus as he reached over the side of his horse and pulled his right boot out of the stirrup before he swung his leg over the horse. Balancing his belly on the saddle, he removed his left foot from the saddle and then dropped onto both feet. She didn't say anything. The cowboy had proved sensitive about his war injury. Apparently he didn't have full use of his right leg and he was embarrassed by the fact.

Once again she hoped he'd have the courage to tell her about it. In the meantime she pulled out the sandwiches. "Hungry?"

ANGUS MOVED SLOWLY, letting his legs adjust to being on the ground after an hour in the saddle. His inner thighs ached a little, but so far the phantom pain remained at bay. He could handle sore muscles much easier than the other.

He accepted the sandwich Reggie offered and peeled back the cellophane to reveal thick homemade bread stuffed with chunky slabs of smoked ham.

Reggie perched on a large boulder, letting her

legs dangle over the side. She scooted over and patted the space beside her. "Sit."

He shook his head. "I'd rather stand."

"Sore?" she asked, taking a bite out of her sandwich.

"A little," he admitted. "But it feels good to be back in the saddle."

"I know what you mean. When I went away to college in Boulder, I missed riding and being in the mountains. I couldn't wait for summer break to get back home."

"I can imagine. This is a great place to come home to."

"That's why I'll never sell." Reggie stared out across the valley. "I want Tad to continue to have this place to call home."

While Reggie stared out at the landscape, Angus studied her. The woman had great passion for the ranch and for the mountains, and she was a fighter. She'd let nothing get in the way of her desire and determination to preserve her son's heritage.

"How did your husband die?" Angus asked and immediately regretted it when Reggie's forehead furrowed and her blue eyes darkened. "Don't answer, if it hurts too much still."

She stared down at the sandwich in her hand for a long moment before she looked up again.

"It's okay. He's been gone a year. I've accepted he's not coming back."

"You must have loved him a lot."

"Yes. I did." Her eyes glazed.

His heart squeezed so hard it ached. To be loved that deeply was a gift. He hoped Ted had appreciated it while he was alive.

Reggie shook herself and the glaze of tears cleared. "It's just hard to talk about it when we're out here. You see, he was thrown from his horse at the top of the ridge we just went over."

Angus glanced back the way they'd come at the stark, sheer cliff they'd passed on the trek across the ridge, and his heart skipped several beats. No one would have survived a fall over that. Now he understood why she'd paused at that point, her face blanching white. She'd been reliving that moment in her life when her world had fallen along with her husband.

Reggie went on, her sandwich forgotten. "I was in town when the accident occurred, meeting with the school about enrolling Tad in kindergarten. CW had gone out riding with Ted that day." Her voice cracked. "Poor CW. He saw it happen. He watched Ted fall to his death and could do nothing about it."

Angus knew what it felt like to watch someone you cared about die and be helpless to keep it from happening. He could understand CW's protectiveness toward Reggie. The man probably felt in some way responsible for the death of the woman's husband and would do anything to make sure she had everything she needed and the protection she deserved.

Angus still carried the guilt of surviving when other members of his unit had died in the IED explosion that had claimed his leg.

"CW had been beside himself when he finally made it back to the ranch. Jo called for help, but by the time it arrived, it was too late. The emergency personnel who'd retrieved his body from the bottom of the cliff said he'd died on impact. No matter how quickly anyone could have come, he would not have survived."

"I'm sorry for your loss."

"Yeah." She rewrapped the remainder of her sandwich and stood. "We love, we lose and we get on with life as best we can."

Angus repackaged the other half of his sandwich and handed it to her. She tucked the sandwiches in the saddlebag and pulled out two bottles of water, handing one to him.

When their fingers touched, a shock of electricity zipped up his arm.

Reggie's eyes widened. She must have felt it, too.

For a moment Angus stared down into her blue eyes, caught in their sadness. He found himself wanting to make them brighten. "Your husband was a very lucky man."

"How can you say that? He died."

Angus nodded. "But while he lived, he had you."

Her lips twisted. "I'm no prize."

"You're wrong." He reached up with his free hand and brushed a strand of hair out of her face. "You're beautiful, courageous...and you're deeply passionate."

Her cheeks reddened and she glanced away. "If this is about that kiss..."

"No, darlin'. And yes." He tipped her chin up, forcing her to look into his eyes. "You have passion for what you believe in. And that passion fills every corner of your life."

As she stared into his eyes, he couldn't help himself. They were so close. If he bent just a little, he could kiss her again as he had in the kitchen.

Her tongue slipped out to wet her lips, the motion pushing him past rational thought. Instinct made him lower his head, his mouth hovering over hers. As before, he gave her the option to retreat if she wanted to. He held his breath, praying she wouldn't, when she had every right to. They'd been talking about her dead husband. A woman would be crazy to kiss another man after that.

"Why are you making this so difficult?" she

whispered. Then, with her free hand, she curled her fingers into his jacket, dragged him closer and leaned up on her toes at the same time to close the distance between them.

When her lips met his, all bets were off. He couldn't have held back if enemy guns were pointed at him. His arms closed around her, pulling her body against his, and he cursed the layers of clothing between them.

His hands curved around her cheeks and swept across her ears to the back of her head as he deepened the kiss, his tongue slipping past her teeth to slide across her tongue.

A soft moan rose up her throat and into his mouth. His groin tightened and he pressed closer. If the air wasn't so danged cool…if they weren't pressed for time…if their timing wasn't so lousy.

Alas, what started as a kiss was destined to end as one. Reluctantly, Angus pulled away and leaned his forehead against hers. "You are a beautiful woman and there is so much more I'd like—"

She touched a finger to his lips and stepped back. "Don't. I'm already struggling to understand what just happened. Can we forget about it for now?" Her cheeks were flushed, her eyes shining.

He wanted to pull her into his arms and kiss her all over again. "You're right. We have work to do."

"Work. That's why we're here." Her hands dropped to her sides and her tongue skimmed her lips as she gathered their water bottles, careful not to touch his hand again. Then she stowed the bottles, took up her reins and mounted her gelding. Without waiting for him, she nudged her horse into a trot and left Angus standing beside the creek.

Still bothered by the kiss, Angus was slower to follow suit, though he wouldn't let her out of his sight. He fit his boot into the stirrup and swung his leg over the top. Bending forward, he pushed the boot on his prosthetic leg into the other stirrup, reminding himself of the folly of kissing the ranch owner. Not only was he not the right man for her, she'd clearly loved her husband and he wouldn't have a chance competing with a ghost.

With a sigh, he rode off after the doggedly determined woman. She was tough, but her lips were as tender and soft as her skin.

THEY SPENT THE next hour scouring the hillside, bushes and bramble for the scattered cattle. When they had them all together, they herded them toward the mountain trail leading up to the high ridge on the other side.

The clouds had thickened and darkened, blocking out light as if dusk had already set in. Most of the cattle seemed content to follow the single-wide path across the rocky ravine and up the hill. About the time the first steer reached the top of the ridge a cow in the rear bellowed loudly.

An answering bleat echoed from far below.

In the very rear of the formation, Angus heard the sound and turned in his saddle. Far across the narrow valley, on the other side of the creek, stood a solitary calf, perhaps only a month or two old. It bleated again and the cow that had started the communication danced sideways and backward.

"Her calf is back across the valley," Angus called up to Reggie as she struggled to keep her horse on the trail with the cow attempting to back up and turn into them.

Angus backed his horse down the trail to a point he could turn around and descended the path back into the valley. At the bottom of the hill, he waited as Reggie did the same. With the trail finally cleared, the cow raced across the valley and the creek to her calf.

The wind had picked up, whipping the storm clouds into a frothy frenzy. Reggie pulled the collar of her jacket up around her ears as the first drops of frozen rain fell. "We'll have to hurry if we want to get that cow and her calf over the ridge."

The other animals had crossed over and moved out of sight, hopefully descending into the valley beyond. A flash of lightning ripped through the air, followed by the deep, echoing rumble of thunder.

"We're not going up there now. It would be suicide." Angus glanced around, searching for shelter.

"We need to make it to the mine entrance. We can take shelter there until the storm passes," Reggie shouted over the wail of the wind.

Another flash of lightning was followed immediately by the clap of thunder.

Angus's horse danced sideways, tossing his head.

Reggie's horse reared. She hung tight to the saddle and brought her horse under control. The freezing rain turned to sleet, blown sideways like sand blasting at their skin.

Reggie yanked her horse around and rode hard for the mine entrance at the other end of the hillside.

Angus followed, struggling to see as sleet beat against his face and eyes. The horses' hooves slipped and slid over the gravelly slope outside the entrance.

Reggie dropped down out of her saddle, grabbed her reins and his, too, and dragged them in through the gaping black entrance into the darkness. She held the horses while Angus hurried to dismount in his clumsy fashion.

When he was finally on the ground, he glanced back at the weather outside. The sleet was coming down harder, salting the land with tiny white pebbles.

"We can't go much farther into the mine," Reggie said. "It gets so dark you can't see your hand in front of your face, and some of the tunnels have collapsed farther in."

"If we aren't able to get over the ridge tonight, we'll need fuel for a fire," he said. "I'm going out to gather wood."

"I'm going with you," she said. She tied the horses to a boulder and ran out into the storm with him.

The slope proved tricky to Angus, but he gritted his teeth and did his best to remain upright. At the bottom of the hill he hurried toward the brush and fallen timbers, gathering as much kindling as he could. When his arms were full, he headed back to the mine entrance. Reggie was already on her way up. Twice he slipped and dropped his load, but he finally made it up the incline and into the mine.

Reggie stood in the entrance, digging though the saddlebag. "Damn."

"What's wrong?"

"I usually put a box of matches in my saddlebag."

"Not this time?" He wanted to laugh at the look of consternation on her face.

Her shoulders sagged. "No." Then her face

brightened. "You were a Boy Scout. Can't you start a fire without matches or a lighter?"

His lips twitched, but he swallowed the smile threatening to spread across his face. "I could, if I had a flint and a bunch of dryer lint."

"Well, looks like we're going to spend a cold night in this drafty ol' mine." She shivered. "At least we have what's left of our lunch to eat."

"I can do one better than that." He pulled a lighter out of his jeans' pocket. "My dad gave me his lighter when he quit smoking. I carry it as a reminder to value my health."

Reggie's face split in a big smile. "Jerk. Why didn't you tell me in the first place?"

He shrugged. "You didn't ask."

"I asked if you could start a fire."

"Without matches or a lighter," he reminded her.

Her lips twisted and her eyes narrowed. "Are you always this cagey?"

"Only around beautiful women."

"And I'll bet you're quite the charmer around beautiful women," she whispered, staring at him a moment, her gaze slipping to his lips, the cheerful smile disappearing from her face altogether. "Uh, we'd better get that fire going. The temperature is supposed to drop into the teens."

They moved a little farther back in the mine tunnel to avoid the worst of the draft blowing in from the approaching storm.

Angus held up his lighter so that they could see well enough to know what they were stepping into.

Reggie dropped to her haunches and studied a blackened spot on the stone floor. "Looks like someone's been in here recently."

Angus stood over her, staring down at what appeared to be charred remains of a fire. He glanced around the immediate vicinity. "There's some trash against the wall."

Reggie crossed to the wall and toed a candy wrapper and an empty can. "Sometimes kids bring their four-wheelers into the mountains, exploring the trails and old mines."

Angus nodded. He supposed it was possible. He'd loved exploring on horseback when he was a teen, staying gone for hours, sometimes camping out under the stars.

They worked together to stack the wood and kindling into a neat pile with pieces set aside to feed into it later.

"We could use some paper or straw."

Reggie dug into her pocket and pulled out a handful of moss. "This works pretty good."

"Are you always this prepared?"

"I would have been a Boy Scout if I'd been born a boy."

"I, for one, am glad you're not a boy." He bent to set the flame to the moss and pushed it underneath the stack of wood and kindling. Coaxing it along with gentle puffs of air, he soon had flames blazing.

They'd built the fire back far enough from the entrance the wind wasn't as big an issue, but the occasional frigid breeze found its way to their cozy corner.

"Think the storm will blow over soon?" Reggie asked, holding her hands out to the fire, a shiver shaking her body.

"Hard to tell. If it doesn't blow over in the next forty-five minutes, it won't matter. Even if it cleared before dusk, we wouldn't make it over the ridge before dark. I don't know about you, but I don't relish riding the rocky trails at night."

She nodded. "It's not safe." Another shiver racked her frame.

Angus rose and walked over to the horses. He slipped the saddles off, one at a time, laying them on the ground behind Reggie. Then he removed the saddle blankets and returned to her side. Spreading one across the cold, stony, mine floor, he held out his hand. "Sit on that."

"Where will you sit?"

"Leave room for me."

She moved over to one side of the blanket and pulled her knees up to her chin.

Angus lowered himself to the ground, unfolded the blanket and draped it across her lap and his. "Not the best-smelling blanket, but it'll keep us warmer than nothing." He slipped his arm around her.

She leaned against him, stiff at first.

"I'm not going to try anything," he assured her. "But shared warmth will get us through the night."

"I know you're right," she said. "It's just…"

"You're afraid I'll kiss you again?"

"No." She turned her face away and whispered, "I'm afraid *I'll* kiss *you*."

His heart warming at her words, Angus tried not to let it mean too much. When her hand slipped beneath the blanket and across his thigh, he forgot for a moment who he was now. For a brief second he was just a guy holding a girl. Until her calf slid beneath the blanket closer to his. He saw it coming and couldn't move fast enough to stop her.

As her leg touched against the cool hard metal of his prosthetic, Angus froze.

Chapter Nine

In the warmth and strength of Angus's embrace, it only seemed natural and unavoidable for her to slide her leg up against his. She knew, as soon as she did, that there would be no going back. After the kiss, though her skin was cold, the internal fires were raging. She wanted to be with him, to hold him close and to feel his skin against hers.

But when her calf touched his, something wasn't right.

Angus stiffened, his fingers tightening on her arm, his entire body frozen against hers. Even his leg was stiff and as hard as metal and narrow like a pole.

She pressed her knee against his. Instead of soft tissue beneath the denim, it felt more like hard plastic.

"What the hell?" Reggie leaned back, flipped the blanket off and rapped her knuckles against his knee. Then it all hit her with the force of a punch to the gut.

Angus lurched to his feet and walked away.

Reggie sat for a moment, taking in what her head was telling her. "You have a prosthetic leg?"

"Yes," he stated, his back to her, straight and rigid.

"Why didn't you tell me?"

He snorted. "What fool would hire a ranch hand with one leg?"

She laughed, the sound forced and choked on what felt suspiciously like a sob. "You came to the right place. Fool's Fortune." Reggie leaped to her feet and crossed to him, laying a hand on his shoulder. "When I asked what was wrong this morning, why didn't you tell me then?"

He shook off her hand and took another step forward, away from her. "Look, I don't need sympathy or special treatment. I want my work to stand on its own, even if it is on one leg."

"You'll get no argument from me. And I guess I understand your reasons." She crossed her arms. "Still, I don't like being lied to."

"I didn't lie about that." Angus faced her. "I get phantom pain from the nerves that think my leg is still there. I got the injury in the war when the vehicle I was in hit an IED. I lost my leg—all the other men in that vehicle lost their lives." He gripped her arms, his eyes burning with their intensity, reflecting the flames. "I didn't lie."

"Were you afraid I'd see you as less of a man?"

She dared to stare directly into his eyes as she posed the question.

"I can't begin to read your mind." His lips pressed into a tight line. "Now that you know, how *do* you see me?"

"I see a man with a lot to prove." She squared her shoulders and finished. "To himself. I never asked you to prove anything to me, and I wouldn't have. You have a lot more to learn about me than how I kiss."

When she tried to break free of his grip, his fingers tightened and he pulled her against his chest.

She stared up into his eyes. "I know you like to kiss me, or you wouldn't have done it twice."

He shook his head. "I didn't kiss you. You kissed me. But I'm going to kiss you now."

"No, you're n—"

His lips closed over hers in a crushing kiss that stole her breath along with her will to resist. Though she tried, she couldn't tear herself away. She melted against him, her arms circling the back of his neck as his tongue slid along the length of hers.

He didn't stop there, dragging his lips along the line of her jaw to the tender skin below her earlobe.

She tilted her head to the side, allowing him more access to her neck.

He spread more kisses along her neck, his

fingers dragging down the zipper on her coat. Cool air slipped into the warmth of her body.

When she shivered, he stopped. "It's too cold here." He bent and lifted her into his arms and carried her to the blanket in front of the fire where, he lowered her legs, letting her slide down his front until her feet touched the ground.

She finished unzipping the front of her jacket and reached out to his, slowly dragging the zipper down until it hung open. Then she slipped her hand beneath his sweatshirt and tugged the chambray shirt from the waistband of his jeans. She ran her hands up his chest, reveling in the feel of his skin against her fingertips.

He closed his eyes; his fists clenched at his sides.

She could tell he was fighting himself not to touch her, making her want him even more.

When she noticed, she removed her hands from his body, grabbed both of his and slipped them beneath her shirt, guiding them up to her breasts.

His eyes opened and fire burned in their dark depths. "If this is out of pity…"

"It is." When he stiffened, she gave him a half smile and added, "*Self*-pity. It's been a long time since I've let a man other than my husband touch me. I want to feel again." She reached behind her and unclasped her bra, her breasts falling free of the garment into his warm, callused palms.

His fingers closed around them, kneading the flesh. He found and tweaked the tips of her nipples into tight little buds.

Her breath caught in her throat and she arched her back, pressing herself more firmly into his hold. It was beautiful, wonderful, and more magical than she had remembered. But it wasn't enough.

Reggie pressed her hands to the backs of his to stop him. "Wait."

He dropped his hands to his sides and took a step back, shoving a hand through his hair. "I shouldn't. We shouldn't."

"I didn't say stop. I said wait." She lowered herself to her knees and reached for his hand.

He hesitated. "I haven't been with a woman since…"

"And I haven't been with a man since…" She laughed softly. "I think that makes us even."

For another long moment he stared at her. Then he lowered himself to sit beside her and pulled her into his arms. "Are we a pair of misfits?"

"Maybe, but I'm not settling for less than the whole enchilada."

She pushed his jacket over his shoulders and it fell to the ground behind him. Then she removed her jacket and yanked her sweatshirt up over her head, her unclasped bra coming off with it. Sitting beside him with only her jeans on, she shivered. "Now it's your turn."

He yanked his sweatshirt off and practically ripped the buttons off his shirt trying to get it open fast enough.

Once he'd shed the shirt, she could see the scars across his chest and torso, and her heart bled for the man. She refused to show him any sympathy, knowing it would hurt him more than the wounds. Instead she traced each one with her fingertips. "Was it bad in the war?"

His body grew rigid. "It wasn't a picnic."

Her chest tightened. She could only imagine the horrors he'd lived through. "I think your scars give you more character," she murmured.

"To hell with character," he growled, laying her down on the blanket as close to the crackling fire as they could get to take advantage of the warmth while they lay half-naked in the freezing cold. He dragged the other blanket up over their shoulders and lay beside her, skimming the back of his hand across her chin and down the path his lips had taken moments before.

Her skin tingled everywhere he touched. Despite the cold, her body burned and her blood hummed to life in her veins.

Angus brushed his lips over her collarbone and downward, capturing the peaked tip of one nipple between his lips and rolling it between his teeth, nibbling and flicking it with his tongue.

Reggie moaned and threaded her hands in his

hair, guiding him to the other breast, which he treated with the same sensual attention.

Breathless and ready to take the next step, she reached between them and undid the button on her jeans.

"Uh-uh." Angus's voice rumbled against her skin and he brushed her hands away, replacing them with his own. He dragged her zipper down and slid his hand into the elastic band of her panties, cupping her sex.

Her knees parted and she raised her hips, urging him closer.

Angus's mouth moved from her breasts down her rib cage and across her belly, stopping where his hand disappeared inside her panties.

Her breathing grew shallow; her heart rattled in her chest and her belly clenched.

"Say the word and it stops here," he said, his breath warm against her skin.

With the fire warming her side closest to the flame, another flame flared deep inside.

"Please," she said.

He blew out another breath, sending tingles to her core.

"Don't stop," Reggie whispered.

His finger slid between her folds and stroked her there, at the most sensitive part of her body.

Reggie whimpered.

"Am I hurting you?"

"Oh, yes." Her voice caught. "In the best way."

She didn't even sound like herself, her words coming out breathy, her lungs unable to capture enough oxygen while he played her like a musical instrument.

He stroked her again, igniting her nerves, the sensations rocketing through her like so many jagged bursts of lightning across the sky.

When he took his hand away, she almost cried out, until he slipped her jeans down over her hips and pulled them off with her boots, laying them aside but near the fire to keep them warm.

She leaned forward and flicked the button loose on his jeans and pushed at them, wanting to see more of his warrior body.

He helped her ease his jeans lower, but stilled her hands when they were halfway down his thighs. The man was tough, a hard-core soldier, but when it came to revealing his injury, he had a long way to go.

Reggie didn't push the issue. In time, he might trust her enough to reveal all, but for now she had what she wanted.

His member jutted out; hard, long and thick.

Her fingers wrapped around it, feeling it pulsing against her palm, and her confidence soared. She slid her hand down his length, reveling in the heat and strength of his desire. Wanting him, inside her…now…she gave him a gentle tug, guiding him to her entrance.

Angus pulled back slightly, refusing to take it to the next level.

Reggie's gaze met his in the soft glow from the fire.

"Protection."

Her eyes widened. Why hadn't she thought of it? "I don't have anything."

"In the back pocket of my jeans, in my wallet."

She reached around him, her hands skimming over his naked butt, triggering a warm flush of pure lust. The urgency more potent, she fumbled in his back pocket, found his wallet and searched through it until she found a foil packet.

With a rush of relief, she folded his wallet, returned it to this back pocket and ripped open the foil packet.

At that moment a blast of cool air found its way into the mine, along with the whistling wail of the wind. A tremor shook her body and she hesitated.

"We don't have to do this." Angus bent to kiss her lips, his tongue slipping between her teeth.

With his big body blocking the cool air, she warmed again. "No. I want this." Quickly, before she could change her mind, she rolled the condom over his engorged shaft. Then she guided him to her damp entrance.

He dropped down on his elbows, his big, warm body covering hers as he slid into her.

Reggie raised her knees and lifted her hips, urging him deeper.

The heat of the fire had nothing on the scorching flames burning inside.

With each of his thrusts, she met him, increasing in speed and urgency. He was so thick he stretched the walls of her channels deliciously, filling that empty, needy space.

Tingling sparks ignited in her center, spreading outward. She jammed her heels into the ground and pushed upward as he thrust deeper.

Her breath caught and held as she rode wave after wave of sensation, his member pulsing inside her. When she finally came back to earth, she lay limp against the blanket, her body used up and worn out by the intensity of their lovemaking. Yet, if he indicated he wanted to do that again, she knew her stamina would revive and she'd be up for it.

Angus rolled onto his side, pulled her back against his front and dragged the saddle blanket up over them. Then he draped his arm around her middle, his hand fondling her breast, his breath stirring the hairs around her ear.

"You're not only beautiful, you're amazing," he whispered, kissing the sensitive spot beneath her earlobe.

With the heat of his body behind her and the fire warming her face, she closed her eyes. Tomorrow would be soon enough to allow reason to return. Tomorrow she might regret what happened in the mine. But at that moment she refused to consider the future. Living in the here and now, with Angus's strong arms around her, she slept.

ANGUS LAY AWAKE into the night, listening to the sound of Reggie breathing. Making love to her had been so incredible, his heart was still racing and he struggled to think past her bare bottom pressed against his groin. After his injury and all the hours he'd spent in rehabilitation, he'd wondered if he'd lost the ability to make love with a woman.

A mix of awe and elation filled him. Awe for how good it had felt to be inside Reggie, her inviting him in, squeezing tightly around him. And elation for discovering that, though he'd lost his leg, he hadn't lost other functionality.

As his pulse slowed and he came back to his senses, he had to tell himself not to get too attached. He was the hired hand. Hell, he was her undercover bodyguard. Surely there were rules about falling in love with the person you were supposed to protect.

When the threat to her and the Last Chance Ranch was neutralized, he'd have to move on. Where to? He didn't know. Hank would send him off on another assignment and Reggie would be on her own on this big ol' ranch, taking care of everything with only the help of CW.

What would have happened to her if she'd been up in the high country by herself? Would she have gotten a fire going or struggled to stay alive through freezing temperatures on her own? If her horse had thrown her, it would have been hours, maybe days, before someone found her. She'd have died in the extreme temperatures.

A heavy weight settled against his chest.

Walking away from Reggie would be a lot harder than he'd originally thought when he'd first showed up at the ranch.

The woman was strong, determined, and cared about her son and the Reinhardts, whom she treated as extended members of her family.

Hell, if she couldn't afford to pay a ranch hand she desperately needed, she probably couldn't afford to pay an old man and his wife to continue working on the ranch.

Being softhearted didn't make good business sense, but it made Reggie the kind of person Angus feared he could easily fall in love with.

Tomorrow he'd do some more digging around, report in to Hank and give him the name of the only potential suspect. Hank would pass the information to his computer guru, who would run the name and see what came up. And somehow he'd overnight the board to wherever Hank had latent prints analyzed.

He had to focus on protecting Reggie. Getting involved would derail him from accomplishing the mission.

But for that moment, he told himself, he couldn't move away from her. And, Lord knew, he didn't want to. She needed his warmth. Almost as much as he needed hers.

Chapter Ten

A cold draft nudged Reggie awake the next morning. She rolled onto her back and stretched, the coarse blanket abrading her tender breasts. Her eyes popped open and she stared down at the saddle blanket covering—she looked beneath it—her naked body.

She sat up with a jerk and yanked the blanket to her neck. Holy hell, what had she done? And where was Angus?

The man on her mind stepped into the mine chamber and leaned against the timbers holding up the ceiling. "If you're looking for your clothing, it's down by your feet."

"Why didn't you wake me?" Reggie said, feeling with her hand beneath the blanket for her shirt and jeans.

"I didn't see any need to wake you. I took my horse out past the creek to see what the trail conditions were."

Reggie found her bra and slipped the blanket

over her head while she dressed in her bra and shirt. When she was covered on top, she tugged the blanket down to her waist. "And what are the trail conditions?" she asked, avoiding mention of the previous night.

"We should be okay getting the cow and calf up over the ridge if we hurry."

"More weather headed our way?" she asked as she dragged her jeans over her hips, tugging at the blanket as it got caught in the process.

"Clouds are hanging low over the hills and there were patches of icy mist."

"Then we'd better get going." Reggie flung the blanket off, pulled her boots on and stood.

Angus bent to retrieve the saddle blankets, shook them out, and a pair of black, lacy, bikini panties fell to the ground.

Her cheeks heating, Reggie snatched the panties up in her hand and tucked them into her pocket. She then slipped her arms into her jacket, pulling it tight around her.

The fire had burned down to nothing but glowing coals, the heat dissipating as the coals cooled.

Her stomach grumbled loudly as she gathered her saddle.

Angus laid the folded blanket on her gelding's back. "Let me get that." When he reached for the saddle, she didn't argue. Stiff from the cold and hungry, she just wanted to get back to the ranch house and take a hot shower. But they still had at least a few hours of riding before they saw breakfast. Half a sandwich for lunch and dinner didn't go far.

Her stomach growled again. This time she was certain Angus heard. If she wasn't mistaken, his lips had twitched.

"If it makes you feel any better, I'm hungry, too." He cinched the saddle, dropped the stirrup in place and then bent to give her a leg up. "The sooner we get this job done, the sooner we can fill our bellies."

Thankful he hadn't mentioned what had happened the night before, she planted her foot in his laced hands and mounted her horse.

He remained standing beside her, even after she was seated. His gaze met hers. "About last night."

The bottled-up nerves released in a short burst of laughter. "Sounds like a line from a book or movie." Reggie raised her hand. "I'd rather not talk about it."

"It shouldn't have happened."

"People make mistakes when it's dark and cold. Let's leave it at that."

He nodded, his lips thinning. "A mistake."

"Right." She couldn't meet his gaze, lifting hers to stare out at the gray sky. The low ceiling of clouds reflected how she felt. He'd agreed what had happened was a mistake. Reggie should be relieved. Instead she wanted to cry.

She waited as he mounted his horse, trying not to stare while he tucked his boot into the right stirrup. For a man missing a leg, she'd never have known if she hadn't forced the issue last night with a simple touch.

Oh, and where that simple touch had led. Her face burning, she nudged her horse forward, exiting the mine. The slope was slippery, her horse's hooves, sliding in the gravel on the descent. When she reached the bottom, she headed toward the cow and her calf, grazing down by the creek.

Between her and Angus, they closed in on the cow and calf, urging them to cross the creek and make for the trail to the top of the ridge.

The calf broke away several times, bucking and kicking up its heels. Each time, Angus or Reggie cut it off, sending it back to its mother.

The cow plodded along, bellowing to the calf. Eventually the cow started up the trail and the calf fell into step behind her.

In less than thirty minutes they'd topped the ridge and started down the other side. This time Reggie didn't pause and didn't let herself think about the location of her husband's fall. She was too busy worrying about Angus and how she'd manage to continue on as if what happened the night before had never occurred.

Once they reached the meadow, Angus and Reggie split up, each taking one side, herding the stragglers into a semblance of a formation. When they had them all together, they moved them toward the trail home, the first snowflakes drifting down from the sky.

The going was slow, with the occasional rebel breaking formation in an attempt to get back to the meadow. Reggie and Angus refused to let them. Tiny white flakes grew bigger and thicker as dark gray clouds settled low over the hills.

Reggie hunkered down in her coat, pulling her collar up around her ears and her wool scarf over the top of her head, tucking it into her jacket. She wished she'd thought to wear a cowboy hat. Every few minutes, she shook the accumulated snow off her scarf.

"Want my hat?" Angus asked.

"No, I can manage," she said, the cold pushing through her clothing, making her shiver.

The cattle no longer tried to get away, settling into a steady march toward the lower pastures.

The slow pace gave Reggie too much time to think about what she'd say to Angus when they got back to the barn. Ignoring the issue wouldn't make it go away. What they'd shared couldn't happen again. She had a young son to consider. How would Tad react to someone kissing his mother or touching her in an intimate fashion?

Not that it would happen again. First of all,

Angus would have to want to. Second, she'd have to let him. Reggie refused to succumb to lust again. That's all it had been. She barely knew the man. How could it be anything else? In her experience, relationships were built over time and mutual respect, not with hormones and primal instinct.

By the time the rocky trail leveled into the lower, flatter pastureland, the snow was falling so fast it was like thick lace she could barely see through. If she hadn't been so familiar with the terrain and if the cattle hadn't had some kind of internal homing instinct, they might have wandered off course. She caught a glimpse of the shadowy shape of the barn. The cattle already in the pasture called out to those on their way in and the herd picked up the pace. Soon they were galloping toward the gate.

Reggie let her horse have its head and raced ahead to open the gate, glad snow covered the ground and any potential fake snakes. She leaned over in the saddle and opened the gate, pushing it wide. Then she backed her horse to the side, watching to ensure the penned cattle didn't come out while the stragglers went in.

Angus followed the herd until all the animals passed through the gate. Reggie dismounted and closed the gate behind the errant calf and cow that had delayed their return to the house by a day.

CW emerged from around the side of the barn, his wrinkled face creased in a smile. "You two don't know how relieved I am to see you."

"Almost as relieved as we are to see you?" Reggie smiled at the older man and hugged him. "We were delayed by a cow, her calf and a storm."

"I know you told me not to worry and that you'd hole up in the mine if you ran into trouble, but..." He ran his gloved hand over his face, the lines etched even deeper than they had been the day before. "I couldn't help thinking."

"CW, you can't keep worrying so much about me. I had Angus with me and the mine was warm and dry once we built a fire."

The old man nodded. "I know. But then the snow started falling so thick I couldn't see my hand in front of my face."

"It was pretty bad, but we made it just fine."

"Let me take care of the horses for you." He waited while Angus dismounted and then led the horses into the barn.

Angus and Reggie followed.

"The missus will want to know you're safe."

"CW, how'd Tad do last night?" Ever since her husband died, Tad got worried when Reggie came in later than usual.

"We told him you and Angus was camping out. He seemed okay with that. And we let Ranger sleep in his room." CW glanced at Angus. "I hope you don't mind. The dog was a little antsy when you didn't return, and he seemed to calm Tad. The two of them slept together." CW shook his head. "It was the darnedest thing."

"I don't mind at all," Angus said. "Thank you for taking care of Ranger while I was gone."

"He was no bother. We barely knew he was there. And Tad has taken a likin' to the animal. He fed him and gave him fresh water."

"I'm glad." Reggie said. "Thank you for keeping his routine."

CW nodded. "I was gonna call the sheriff at noon if you two hadn't showed up by then."

"What time is it?"

"A quarter to noon." CW took in a deep breath and let it out, then turned to Angus. "It's a good thing you were out there with Ms. Reggie."

"I'd have been fine on my own," Reggie insisted.

"I know. But it's better to have backup in case something goes wrong."

Like forgetting the matches. Reggie shot a glance at Angus, wondering if his thoughts had gone in the same direction.

His expression remained unreadable.

"Go on. I got the horses. You two need to check in with Jo before she makes that call." CW waved them toward the barn door. "Ranger is on the back porch. I think he's been waiting for you to come home."

Reggie was silent as they crossed the yard to the house.

Ranger stood on the back porch, his tail wagging his entire body as Angus approached.

Angus sat on the steps, wrapped his arms around the dog's neck and hugged him.

The big man's happiness at seeing his dog touched Reggie more than she cared to admit. Despite the cold, her hunger and the snow accumulating on her, Reggie stared at the picture the man and dog made together.

When Angus straightened, the three of them entered the house through the kitchen door.

As soon as she stepped through, Reggie could smell Jo's famous pot roast. Her stomach growled and she almost felt sick with hunger.

Jo wasn't in the kitchen and when Reggie called out, it was a few seconds before the older woman responded.

"Reggie, honey? Is that you?" She hurried into the kitchen, a worried expression clearing when she saw Reggie. She folded her into her arms and hugged her tight. "Oh, thank goodness. I was just telling William we were about to call the sheriff to send out a rescue team to find you and Angus." She turned and hugged Angus, too.

"Will's here?" Reggie asked.

"Yes, dear. I'm going to go fill the bathtub for you. You must be dead tired after camping out all night." As Jo turned to leave the kitchen, Reggie caught sight of her brother.

William Coleman, her younger brother, entered the kitchen, handsome in a tailored suit, his hair neatly combed to one side. On his arm was Lillian Kuntz, one of his coworkers at the real estate agency in Fool's Fortune.

"Hello, Regina," Lillian said. She wore a dark gray herringbone pantsuit with a powder blue sweater and a string of pearls around her neck. The woman never had a hair out of place and her clothes clung to her body as if they were tailor-made. She smiled brilliantly with her perfectly whitened teeth and held out her hand to Angus. "We haven't met. I'm Lillian Kuntz, Will's fiancée."

Angus shook her hand. "Angus Ketchum. Pleasure to meet you."

Reggie blinked, feeling as if she'd been sucker punched. "Fiancée?" She stared from Lillian to William and back.

Lillian held up her left hand. On her ring finger was a shiny brand-new marquise diamond engagement ring. She curled her arm through Will's. "Will popped the question while we were in Denver having dinner at our favorite Italian restaurant."

William's cheeks reddened. "I was going to tell you, but we'd been so busy lately and...well..." He shrugged. "I wasn't sure she'd say yes."

"Silly man. How could he not know how much I love him?"

Reggie nodded at the *silly man*. Her only adult, living relative had gotten engaged and she hadn't known it was even going to happen.

Then again, she hadn't been a big fan of Lillian Kuntz. Reggie had suspected her brother was falling for his coworker. She'd hoped he'd get over it and find a nicer woman, better suited to him.

Reggie, feeling even dirtier and more rumpled than before, forced a smile. "I guess congratulations are in order." When Lillian wasn't looking and Will was, she mouthed the words "we'll talk later."

Will nodded, covering Lillian's hand with his and tipped his head toward Angus. "I know his name is Angus, but who is he?"

Reggie hesitated a moment, then rushed to answer. "The new ranch hand."

Will grinned. "Glad you finally got more help. This place is too big for you."

"Not at all," she said. "Now, if you'll excuse me, I'd like to clean up. We got caught out in the storm last night."

Will glanced toward the window. "You were out in that mess? You could have died of exposure."

"Yeah, well, we didn't." She shoved her hand through her dirty, tangled hair.

"When are you going to sell this ranch?" William asked. "Ted couldn't have expected you to run it by yourself. It's too much."

Reggie's mouth tightened into a firm line. "We've had this discussion before."

"I know we have. But I won't always be around to help out. With my sales rising, I'll be busier than ever. And when Lillian and I get married… well, I'll have other priorities."

"You will, won't you, darling?" Lillian leaned into him and stared across at Reggie. "Really, Regina, you should consider selling this big place. I'm sure we could come up with several really nice offers. You and Teddy could find a nice little house in town and not have to worry about fences falling down or a storm shutting you off from the rest of the world."

"Tad," Reggie corrected her. "Thank you, Lillian. But I'm not interested."

"It's just foolish to continue trying to run this ranch," Lillian started. "It can't possibly be making enough income to sustain you and Teddy."

Reggie fought to control her anger. "Tad," she corrected Lillian again.

Will leaned toward his fiancée. "Reggie's son's name is Tad."

Lillian gave him an irritated look. "Oh, yes, of course. Regina, surely you see keeping Tad hidden away on a ranch so far out in the country, you're not giving him all the opportunities he could have in town."

Will's hand tightened on hers. "Lillian—"

The woman raised her free hand. "Let me finish."

Reggie clenched her fist, her first instinct to punch the woman in the face for her rudeness to her brother. "Lillian, I think you *are* finished."

Chapter Eleven

Angus recognized the color rising in Reggie's cheeks. If he wasn't hungry and in need of a shower, he might consider letting the battle between Will's fiancée and Reggie continue. But he was getting irritated with the woman's persistence and the conversation had long since reached its limit.

"Ms. Kuntz, I believe Reggie has stated her desire not to sell. Now excuse us while we go clean up." He hooked Reggie's elbow and led her past Lillian and Will toward the back of the house.

"Don't worry about us," Lillian said airily. "Will was just going to show me the wine cellar."

"Reggie, you don't mind if we find a bottle of champagne to celebrate our engagement, do you?" Will asked.

Reggie dug her feet in, resisting Angus's attempt to get her out of striking range of William's fiancée. As Angus hustled her out of the kitchen, she muttered, "I don't mind William taking a bottle, but I'll be damned if I let that witch—"

Leaning close to her ear so that only she would hear, Angus whispered, "Scrambled eggs, bacon and biscuits."

A loud rumble from her belly indicated he'd made his point.

Jo found Reggie and Angus in the hallway. "I've filled the bath for you, Ms. Reggie. I'll have breakfast for the two of you when you're done."

"What about that pot roast I smelled?" Angus asked.

Jo grinned. "You can have lunch right after you have breakfast, if you like."

"I just might. After I get cleaned up." Angus smiled at the older woman. "Thank you, Mrs. Jo."

Reggie's arm relaxed in Angus's grip. Halfway down the hall, she spoke. "Thanks. If you hadn't gotten me out of there, I'm afraid I'd have ripped Lillian's face off."

Angus nodded. "She's not worth it."

"How can my brother consider marrying someone like that?" She glanced back over her shoulder as if to study the woman in question, who was no longer in sight. "She's all wrong for him."

"Perhaps he sees more in her than you do."

Reggie snorted. "If he'd start thinking with his head instead of his pants, he might figure it out."

"Love can be blind," Angus offered.

"And some say too much sex can make you *go* blind."

Angus stopped in the middle of the hallway and burst out laughing. "I can't believe you just said that."

Her lips twitched at the corner, though she seemed to be fighting the urge to laugh. "Okay, so they said that in high school. If the shoe fits the situation, let it be worn."

"Go get your bath." He gave her a gentle push toward her bedroom. "You'll feel much better about everything when you're clean and fed."

"I doubt it," she grumbled.

Angus stood with his arms folded across his chest until Reggie gave up and entered her bedroom, closing the door behind her.

Angus entered his room, Ranger on his heels. Gathering clean clothing and his toiletries, he crossed the hall to the bathroom, stripped, removed his prosthetic leg and hopped into the shower. Even while making love with Reggie, he hadn't stripped completely naked. He wondered how she'd feel if she saw him like this.

What did it matter? They'd never make love again. She wasn't interested, and his time on the Last Chance Ranch was limited to solving the mystery of who was causing all the trouble.

When he stepped into the hallway twenty minutes later, he was a little disappointed he didn't run into Reggie. But then, Jo had said something about filling a bath for her. An image of her lying naked in a bathtub flashed through Angus's mind and his groin tightened. Images of her naked body bathed in firelight filled his mind. He'd have a hell of a time forgetting that image. Being around her day in and day out would only make it worse.

The sooner he figured out who was causing problems on the ranch, the sooner he'd be out of Reggie's life and he could start the process of forgetting her. If he ever did.

In the meantime he had work to do to end this assignment and move on. He headed for the kitchen, hoping he'd catch Jo or CW.

Jo was alone at the stove. She turned when he entered the room. "Oh, good. I was just about to pop some eggs in the skillet for you. How do you like them?"

"Thank you, Mrs. Reinhardt. Could you hold off for a minute? I need to make a phone call."

"Sure. You'll probably want to eat with Ms. Reggie. Her bath will take a bit longer than a shower."

"Is there a phone I can use?"

She nodded to the one on the counter. "That one right there."

"Is there one a little more private?" He leaned

closer to Jo. "I don't want Reggie or her brother to overhear my conversation."

"Oh, okay. You can use the one in the study."

Angus hurried to the study, wanting to get the call out of the way before Reggie emerged from her bath. He didn't like keeping things from her, but he didn't want her to boot him off the property when she had someone clobbering her in the head with a two-by-four.

He lifted the receiver and punched the numbers for Hank Derringer. Two rings and a male voice answered. "CCI, Brandon speaking."

Brandon Pendley was the computer genius Hank had hired to perform all things geek related, from setting up security systems to hacking into government databases.

"Brandon, it's Angus. Is Hank around?"

"Sure, let me get him."

"Before you go, let me give you some names to check up on."

"Shoot."

"Look up Vance Peterson and Daniel Freeman."

"Got it."

Angus hesitated then added, "Also, Lillian Kuntz."

"Got 'em. Oh, and here's Hank."

"Thanks, Brandon."

"Angus." Hank's cheerful voice came on the line. "How's it going in Colorado?"

He filled Hank in on what he'd learned so far and what had happened to Reggie in the two days he'd been there, excluding his lapse of self-control when making love with Reggie in the mine.

"Sounds like CW called it right," Hank said. "I'm glad you're there to help Ms. Davis and her boy. Do you need me to send some backup?"

"No, not yet. Reggie still doesn't know I'm more than just a ranch hand. I'm afraid if I told her now, she'd ask me to leave."

Hank chuckled. "Independent, huh?"

"Yes, sir." Angus knew how difficult it was to run a ranch with a full staff of ranch hands. When he left, she and CW would be back to managing it on their own.

The thought didn't sit well with Angus. But then, he wouldn't be around after they solved the mystery and made the ranch a safe place to live again.

"I gave Brandon some names to look up. Peterson is a speculator out here trying to buy up land for potential mining purposes. Freeman is a local survivalist who has been known to cause some trouble."

"And the woman?"

"Reggie's brother's fiancée." Angus didn't like that he was digging into Reggie's potential family member's background, but somehow he didn't think Reggie would give a damn about it, since it was Lillian. She had no great love for the woman and Angus didn't blame her.

"We'll check into the mining companies in the area, as well, to see if they are known for strong-arm tactics."

"Good. I'll do some more digging in town."

"Most importantly, stay with the woman. If she's been targeted several times, she will most likely be targeted again."

"Will do," Angus said though he'd already had that thought.

"How's the actual ranching going?" Hank asked. "It's like riding a bike, isn't it? Once you learn, it's always with you, no matter what."

Angus realized it was. "Better than I expected." Sure, he'd had to adjust to the loss of one limb, but he could still get around and do almost everything he'd been able to do before. "Thanks for the opportunity, Hank."

"Knew you were the right person for the job the day I met you."

"I don't know about that, but I'll do my best." He admired the billionaire and respected his reasons for starting CCI.

Hank Derringer had told him he only hired cowboys who were honest, trustworthy and who were as determined to fight for truth and justice as much as he was.

Angus hung up the phone, stepped out of the study and ran into Reggie in the hallway.

He teetered and caught her around the waist to get his balance and steady her at the same time.

With her body flush up against him, his groin tightened and he couldn't help fantasizing about her soft skin beneath her clothes. She wore freshly laundered jeans and a soft blue shirt that molded to her body like a second skin. The color brought out the blue in her eyes. Her skin was soft, warm and flushed a pretty pink from her time in the bath.

"What were you doing in the study?" she asked, her voice breathy, so unlike her usual directness.

Guilt stabbed him like a knife. He wanted to tell her the truth, but telling her now would probably just make her mad. "I needed to make a phone call to check in with a friend and let him know I'd made it here okay. Jo suggested I use the phone in the study. I hope you don't mind."

"Not at all." She stared at his arms around her waist. "You can let go of me now. I promise I won't fall."

"Maybe I'm more afraid I will." His statement was all too true. He could very easily fall for this tough-as-nails woman with skin as soft as silk and a heart as big as the state of Texas. His arms tightened around her.

Her eyebrow quirked.

"Sorry." He let go and stepped back. "I believe Jo was about to cook eggs the way you like them."

"Good. I don't know about you, but I'm starving."

Just one more thing he liked about her. She wasn't the kind of woman who was always dieting and picking at her food. She worked hard and burned calories, so she ate well.

There were too many things he liked about her and it was all getting to be too much. He almost turned and walked back into the study to call Hank and ask him to take him off the assignment.

But when Reggie walked toward the kitchen, he followed.

REGGIE HAD SPENT the better part of thirty minutes soaking in the tub, praying she could soak the man right out of her pores. By the time the water cooled, she knew no amount of soaking, scrubbing or washing would get the man out of her mind.

With Ted, she'd felt more of a partner. Angus made her feel more vulnerable. When he'd pulled her into his arms, she knew he was in control and she'd liked it. Who knew the independent Reggie Davis would like a man who could dominate her but chose to treat her like a fragile flower instead?

When Angus crashed into her and subsequently pulled her into his embrace, she'd had trouble breathing. The way he'd looked at her as if she were a tasty morsel to be feasted on one lick at a time, she was almost glad he was holding her up. If he had let go sooner, her knees would have betrayed her and she'd have melted into a puddle of lusty goo at his feet.

Now she couldn't get away fast enough. One more second in his embrace and she'd have kissed him. How embarrassing would that have been? Just because he'd made love to her in the mine didn't mean he wanted to do it again. Especially after they'd both agreed that it was a mistake.

Before she made it into the kitchen, her brother emerged with Lillian. "Reggie, Lillian and I need to get back to town. When you get a chance, stop by the office. I can give you some comps on the value of the Last Chance Ranch."

"I'm not selling."

"At least you'll have an idea of what it's worth so that you can make an informed decision," Lillian said.

Reggie bit down on her tongue to keep from telling the woman to back off before she put her fist through the other woman's face.

Reggie hugged her brother. "I'm glad you're back from Denver. I love you."

"I love you, too, sis." He hugged her hard and set her away from him.

Will and Lillian departed and the house immediately seemed more relaxed.

Reggie wandered toward the living room and the large picture window.

Angus followed.

"I don't know what my brother sees in that woman." Reggie gazed out the window. "Do you find her attractive?"

The corners of Angus's lips twitched. "Are you fishing for a compliment?"

"Oh, hell, no."

"Well, just for the record, I gravitate to women with sandy-blond hair and blue eyes.

The butterflies in her belly fluttered and it was all she could do to keep her focus on the vehicle disappearing down the drive. Reggie hurried into the kitchen to end the conversation.

"Two eggs, sunny-side up." Jo handed her a plate with eggs, toast, bacon and a square of butter.

Despite the knotting in the pit of her belly, her stomach growled. "Thank you, Jo."

"I made yours over easy," Jo said, handing Angus a plate with four eggs and twice as much toast as on Reggie's. "Sit. I'll pour the coffee."

"You don't have to wait on me, Mrs. Jo," Angus said. "I'm perfectly capable of doing things for myself."

"After spending a night out in the cold, you

just sit yourself down and let me take care of you and Reggie."

On her way to the table, Reggie glanced out the window. The snow hadn't let up and the ground was completely covered in at least two inches already.

Angus's hand was on the back of her chair when she reached for it. Their fingers collided and she snapped her hand back.

He pulled the seat out, his lips twitching.

Damned man. He knew she was jumpy around him and it was funny to him. She tucked into her food, cleaning her plate, glad he didn't say anything else to her during the meal. When she was finished, she wiped her lips on a napkin, pushed back from the table and announced, "I'll pick up Tad from school."

Angus stood and carried his plate and hers to the sink. "I'll go with you."

"You don't have to go with me." Reggie gathered the glasses and set them on the counter beside the plates.

"CW is bound to need some supply or other at the hardware store," Jo offered.

"I can get whatever he needs," Reggie insisted. "No use sending Angus all the way to town just for that."

"I don't mind going. In fact, I need to pick up a few personal items at the drugstore. I'm almost out of shaving cream and my razor is dull."

Oh, yeah, she'd felt the bristles of his beard all across her breasts the night before and had loved the way it abraded her skin so deliciously. Heat rose up her neck and suffused her cheeks. Damn the man. Why couldn't she quit thinking about getting naked with him? "Fine," she said and stomped out of the room, madder at herself than at him. "I'm leaving in five minutes," she called over her shoulder. "We're taking my truck. No argument."

Four and a half minutes later she sat in her beat-up farm truck, tapping her fingers on the steering wheel. At least she'd be doing the driving this time. It would give her something to concentrate on rather than the man in the seat next to her.

Angus emerged from the house wearing his cowboy hat, jeans and a faded blue chambray shirt. Tall, dark-haired and more handsome than a man had the right to be. If he didn't limp, she'd never know he had a prosthetic leg. That fact that he did took nothing away from his potent masculinity.

Reggie dragged her gaze away from him and counted horses in the pasture until Angus climbed up onto the passenger seat.

Without a word she drove out of the yard and across the bumpy lane that led to the highway.

"How long has it been since the ranch road has been graded?" he asked.

"Over a year now." The last time it had been touched was when Ted had been alive. He'd always been the one to take care of road maintenance. Reggie had all she could do to keep up with fencing, cutting, baling and hauling hay as well as worming, tagging and castrating the new calves.

"I'll hook up the box blade to the tractor tomorrow and clear the snow as well as smooth the gravel," Angus said.

"I can do that," she said automatically.

"I know you can, but I'm here and I'm not getting paid to sit around and watch you work."

"You're not getting paid at all." Her lips twisted. "I'm not sure I like that. I'm getting ready to run the steers to the auction down in Leadville next weekend. If all goes well, I'll have a little extra cash. I can pay you then."

"I told you. I don't need anything but room and board. I think I'm getting a pretty good deal with Mrs. Jo's cooking."

Reggie's lips quirked upward in a smile. "She is a good cook, isn't she?"

"The best. I can't wait to get back and dig into that pot roast."

In Reggie's peripheral vision, she could see that Angus was staring out the front windshield. It amazed her that they could talk about inane things while ignoring the elephant in the truck with them—the fact that they'd made love.

Then again, making love to her probably meant very little to him. It was just sex. He might have a flock of females waiting for him back in Texas.

Something stabbed her inside at the thought of Angus with another woman. Hell, she'd just met the man! Her husband, whom she'd loved dearly, had only been dead a year.

"Regina?"

Reggie shot a glance at him. "I don't like being called by my given name."

"I noticed." His lips quirked. "Especially by your brother's fiancée."

She cringed. "I know I should be more welcoming, but she got on my last nerve. After being out all night, for her to show up and give me advice on what I should do with my ranch…"

"Still a little riled?" His twitching lips spread into a grin.

Reggie glanced over for the full force of it. Damned if it didn't hit her square in the chest and make her heart squeeze. The man had a killer smile.

She gripped the wheel and tried to focus on the road before she careened off the side and down one of the many dangerous cliffs. "I shouldn't be so hard on her. Will is helpful on the ranch, when he's not tied up with real estate sales. And I'm not sure Lillian has ever lifted a pitchfork, or can tell one end of a horse from another. It's not a crime."

"But you'd prefer she stayed out of your business," he stated.

"Yes. Ted left me the ranch, free and clear. It's Tad's heritage. It's my fiduciary responsibility to ensure he inherits that legacy. If *he* doesn't want it, *he* can sell it."

"Very noble of you. And I get the feeling you'd work your fingers to the bone to make it happen."

Her brow furrowed. "Now you're starting to sound like Lillian."

"The difference is that I see your efforts as heroic. Lillian probably sees them as foolish."

Reggie's frown lifted and she looked across at him again, her estimation of him rising even more. "Thanks."

"Tad's a lucky kid to have a mother as determined as you."

"Sometimes he doesn't think so." She smiled. "When I tell him it's time to brush his teeth or put up his toys."

"But you're there for him."

"Yeah. And I always will be."

They continued toward town in silence for a couple minutes until Angus broke it. "What would happen to Tad and the ranch if you weren't around anymore?"

Reggie turned. "What do you mean?"

"If I hadn't been with you last night and, say… you slipped off a cliff or died of exposure, what would happen to the ranch and Tad?"

Again, her fingers tightened on the steering wheel. "After Ted died, I had a lawyer draw up a will for me. The ranch will go to Tad. As my only living relative, Will would be the executor of the estate until Tad turns twenty-one."

"Is Will on board with that?"

She nodded. "He was there to witness the will."

"Is Lillian okay playing mommy to Tad if you aren't around?"

"I don't know." Her belly knotted at the thought of Lillian anywhere around her son.

"Who stands to gain most by putting you out of the picture?"

Her head whipped around. "What are you saying?"

"Have you been approached by the mining speculators?"

"Yeah, so?" Her heart fluttered. "Do you think someone's trying to kill me off to get to my land?"

"I don't know, but the accidents around your place seem to be targeting you alone."

Reggie swallowed hard. "God, I never put those things together." She shook herself and straightened. "No, I refuse to believe someone would kill me for mineral rights to my property."

"Are you willing to bank on Tad's mother's life?"

Her foot slipped off the accelerator and her heart stood still for a second.

Was she willing to leave Tad an orphan?

Chapter Twelve

Angus hated the anguish in Reggie's eyes. She'd been clinging to the assumption that what had been happening had all been accidents up until that moment.

"Tad needs me," she whispered. "He's already lost one parent. I know Will would love him as much as I do, but…"

"It wouldn't be you," Angus finished for her.

When she continued to drift to a stop in the middle of the road, he asked, "Do you want me to drive?"

"No. No. I can do this." She pressed her foot to the accelerator and the truck jumped forward. She shot a glance at him. "Are you serious? Do you think I could be the target of some conspiracy to get rid of me?"

Angus shrugged. "Some of the accidents could have been benign, like the fake snake in the barnyard. Maybe it was a prank. Maybe it was a ploy to scare you off your property. Or maybe it was meant to cause real harm to you. But whoever hit you in the head in the barn…that was serious."

"But—" she started.

"Reggie, darlin', you were hit. You did not bump your head on something. I saw someone stealing away from the barn that night."

"Okay, so I should be more aware of my surroundings and the possibility I'm being targeted." She sighed. "It all sounds so clandestine. I live in the hills, who would want me dead?"

"I think that's the real question." Angus stared at the town as they got closer. "Who would want you out of the way?"

"If they want the land…" Her eyes widened and she clapped a hand over her mouth. "Tad. Dear God. He'll inherit if I die." Again, her foot left the accelerator and she drifted to a stop in the middle of the highway, her gaze staring straight ahead, her hands gripping the steering wheel so tightly her knuckles turned white. "What if they go after Tad? He's an innocent little boy."

Angus glanced behind them to ensure they wouldn't be run over. The road was clear. "Reggie." When she didn't respond, he laid his hand on her arm. "So far, all the attempts have been on your life. Not Tad's."

"That doesn't mean they won't go after him next." She pressed her foot to the accelerator. "They could be after him right now." The truck's speed increased until they were flying into town.

"You might want to slow down." Angus tensed as they passed the sheriff's office. "You're going ten miles an hour over the speed limit and you're approaching a school zone."

"Damn right I am," she exclaimed. "I've got to get to my son."

"Tad's at school. If anything was wrong," Angus reasoned, "don't you think the school would have notified you by now?"

She eased up on the accelerator. "I suppose. But—"

"He's okay." Angus sat back in his seat. "What we need to do is to ask more questions. Find out who wants your land and why."

"Since we couldn't get hold of the speculator last time we were in town, do you think we might get lucky and catch him this time?" Her lips pressed into a thin line. "Gotta tell you, though, if he's responsible for all this mess, I'll shoot the bastard."

Angus chuckled. "I'm glad you're not armed."

Her mouth quivered and eventually spread into a smile. "God, I hope we're wrong about all this. I have enough to worry about without watching my back every minute."

"I understand."

"We don't have to get to the school for another hour. You said you needed stuff at the drugstore. I need a few groceries."

"I could stand a trip down the grocery aisles."

She frowned his way. "So now you're going to dog my every step?"

He held up his hands in surrender. "A man likes his own kind of snack foods. That's all." The twinge of guilt gnawed at him. But now was not the time to be divisive.

Reggie parked in front of the grocery store and they both got out.

She picked up a shopping cart at the front of the store. While she worked through produce, Angus headed for the snack aisle and selected microwave popcorn and jerky.

He didn't need it, but he wanted to prove he was there for a reason. Items in hand, he met her at the end of the produce aisles and walked with her up and down the remaining rows until she had all the items on the list she'd brought with her.

Their purchases complete, they left the grocery store loaded with bags. As they settled them into the backseat of the truck Angus heard a shout.

"Ms. Davis!"

Angus set the bag he'd been holding on the floorboard and straightened, ready to defend Reggie if necessary.

Reggie nudged him in the side. "That's the mining speculator, Vance Peterson."

"Good," Angus muttered under his breath. "I have some questions for him."

"Ms. Davis." Vance Peterson hurried over to them from a sleek black BMW SUV. "I'm glad I caught you."

Reggie nodded, her smile tight. "Mr. Peterson."

"Have you given my offer any additional thought?"

"Frankly, Mr. Peterson, no." She didn't mince words, but got down to business. "The land is not for sale."

"I understand that, but maybe I didn't make myself clear. You don't have to sell your land."

"That's right." Reggie crossed her arms.

"You can sell the mineral rights. Or you can lease them."

Her head started shaking before the speculator finished his sentence. "Still not interested. I like the land the way it is."

"But, Ms. Davis, they have so many new ways of mining that don't destroy the land."

"Mr. Peterson, Ms. Davis has made herself clear." Angus stepped forward, towering over the much shorter man. "Let me ask you this. Where were you the night before last around seven in the evening?"

The speculator's mouth closed and he glared up at Angus. "Excuse me, but who are you, and what does that have to do with anything?"

"I just need an answer before you talk to Ms. Davis anymore."

"What," the man snorted. "Are you her body-guard or something?"

Angus tipped his chin up and stared down his nose at the speculator. "Or something."

When the man tried to step around him, Angus shifted to the side, blocking his path to Reggie.

Peterson bristled. "My business is with Ms. Davis."

"And my business is to make sure you don't bother her." Angus wouldn't budge.

"Good grief." Reggie touched Angus's arm. "I can do my own talking, thank you."

The speculator smirked at Angus.

"Where were you the night before last around seven o'clock?"

Vance Peterson's brow puckered. "I don't know. Why?"

Reggie tapped her temple. "Think."

He rolled his eyes. "I was probably at the diner. I usually have dinner there, since it has the best food in town. Again, why?"

"Just wondering."

"Is something the matter?"

Reggie shook her head. "No, nothing."

"If you want to discuss mining techniques, I'd be happy to set up a time for you and me to meet. I could come out to your place, if it's more convenient."

"No."

"You'd be a fool not to, Ms. Davis."

She smiled. "I'm in the right town for that."

The man sneered. "Have it your way. But trust me, you'll be sorry if you don't act on this opportunity." Peterson turned and walked away.

Angus clenched his fists and would have gone after the man but for the hand on his arm. "That sounded like a threat to me."

"You have nothing to substantiate it." She nodded toward the diner. "How about we check his reference to the night I was hit in the head?"

Angus stared after the retreating speculator, wanting to go after him and beat a confession out of him. "If he has anything to do with what's been going on, you won't have to kill him." His jaw tightened. "I will."

FOR A MOMENT Reggie forgot she stood in a snowy street, the time ticking away until she had to collect Tad from school. "If we want to check his alibi, we'd better get a move on. School will be out in fifteen minutes."

She studied Angus as he glared at Peterson. Those fists that looked like hammers had been the same hands that had swept across her body, making her blood sing.

"You're right. We need facts." The stiffness eased from Angus's shoulders and he shook himself. He grinned her way. "Alibi, huh? Now who's sounding like an amateur sleuth?"

Her cheeks heated. "Come on, cowboy, we're

wastin' daylight." She climbed into the truck and pulled out of the parking lot, headed toward the diner at the center of the small town.

At the diner she parked, got out and met Angus at the front. "Can I buy you a cup of coffee? I've only had one for the entire day. I'm feeling withdrawals. Unless you're the kind of guy who insists on buying the coffee."

"I'm not that misogynic." He winked. "Coffee would be great."

When she reached for the door, he got there first. "However, I do believe a man should open a door for a lady."

"Let me clear this up for you. I'm a rancher. Gender is not at question here."

"No, it's not." He pulled the door open. "There is no denying that you are all woman."

She frowned as she passed him and entered the diner.

"Now that's a conversation I'd like to get in on." Kitty stood two feet away from the entrance, her hands on her hips.

Reggie's cheeks burned. "You heard that last remark?"

"Oh, yeah." A smile spread across Kitty's face. "What I want to know is why there was any doubt Reggie was a woman?"

"Never was, in my mind." Angus frowned. "Except once, and it was getting dark then, so that doesn't count. Oh, and it didn't take long for me to figure out the truth once she was lying on the ground."

If Reggie's face could get any hotter, it would spontaneously combust. She glanced around the diner, praying no one was listening to their innuendo-heavy conversation.

"Don't worry, we're at the lull before the storm." Kitty hooked Reggie's arm and led her toward the front counter. "The dinner crowd starts trickling in after school lets out. Sit. I just made a fresh pot of coffee."

"Perfect." The sooner Kitty put the cup in front of her the sooner she'd have something to hold on to, to keep from fidgeting.

"What brings you into the diner two times in one week?" Kitty waved a hand. "Not that I'm complaining. Definitely improves the view." She winked at Angus.

Reggie's blood pressure increased. How did Kitty do that? She was so good at flirting. Hell, she flirted with all her customers—male and female. Reggie just wished she wouldn't flirt with Angus.

"Were you working two nights ago around seven o'clock?" Reggie asked.

Kitty snorted. "I swear I work twenty-four-seven. Of course I was working that night. Can't find enough reliable help." She set a mug in front of Reggie and one in front of Angus and grabbed the coffeepot from the burner.

"Do you happen to recall Vance Peterson coming in that night?" Reggie asked.

Kitty paused before pouring coffee into Reggie's mug. "The man is like clockwork. He's in here every night between six-thirty and seven-thirty." She closed her eyes. "He has our special every night. Two nights ago it was meatloaf. And, yes, he was here." She opened her eyes with a smile. "I remember because he commented that it tasted just like his mother used to make." She glanced from Reggie to Angus as though she'd won a prize. "Why do you ask?"

Reggie turned and parted her hair over the goose-egg-sized bump. "Nothing fell on me in the barn. I got whacked in the head."

"Oh, my God." Kitty set the coffeepot on the burner and rounded the counter to get a closer look at Reggie's forehead. "Someone did this to you?" She reached out to touch her softly. "Who? I'll kill him."

Reggie laughed. "Get in line."

"What happened? Where?" Kitty shook her head. "Why would someone do that?"

"That's what we're trying to figure out," Angus said.

"Tell me all about it," Kitty demanded.

While Kitty hurried around the counter again to pour coffee into both cups, Reggie filled her in on what had been happening.

"You thought Vance might have done it?" Kitty asked.

Reggie sighed. "I don't know who else would want me dead."

"Good Lord." Kitty covered her hand. "I can't imagine anyone wanting my sweet Reggie dead. You wouldn't hurt a fly."

"I'm not sure it's my character they're trying to destroy."

"It could be possible that someone wants to either scare her off or kill her to get to her land."

"For the mining potential?" Kitty's eyes widened. "That sounds so Wild West."

"Tell me about it." Reggie sipped her coffee. "The troubles didn't start until after the speculators came around asking us if we wanted to sell our land or our mineral rights."

"Have you checked in with any of your neighbors to see if they've had similar issues?" Kitty tapped her chin. "What about Chase Marsden? He's right next door."

"Not yet, but that's a good idea." Reggie sipped her coffee. "I wonder if he's been targeted."

Kitty shivered. "Now you're giving me the creeps. How can people look at themselves in the mirror in the morning? Want me to bring my shotgun and stay out at the ranch with you?"

"No." Reggie's lips twisted. "I have CW, Jo and Angus to help me. And I'm a pretty good shot."

"That's the spirit. This means war." Kitty pumped her arm.

Reggie stared into her coffee. "I just hope Tad doesn't get caught in the crossfire." She slid off the stool. "Speaking of which…school will be out in a few minutes. I need to pick him up."

"I'd talk to some of your neighbors," Kitty reiterated. "As for Vance, he was here the night you were attacked. But that doesn't mean he's not responsible. He could have hired someone to do it for him."

Reggie tilted her head. "I hadn't thought of that. For that matter, anyone could have a valid alibi if they hired someone else to take care of me."

Once again Kitty walked around the counter, this time to hug Reggie. "Give Tad a big ol' hug from Auntie Kitty."

"You bet."

"You should bring him by and let me treat him to a milkshake."

"We still have so much to do before it gets dark, or I would." Reggie turned to Angus. "Ready?"

"I am." Once again, Angus beat her to the door and opened it for her.

"A girl could get used to that," she said as she passed through.

"That's right, Angus. Remind her that she is

a woman. I think she forgets sometimes," Kitty called out.

Mortified, Reggie glared back at her friend. "You are not helping."

"Oh, really?" Kitty batted her eyelashes. "And here I thought I was." With a big wink, she flounced back to the kitchen.

"Sorry," Reggie muttered. "Kitty fancies herself the local matchmaker even more than Jo."

"I've noticed that some married women seem to think their single friends should be happily married like them."

Reggie rolled her eyes. "Kitty's not married. Unless you count being married to her work. She owns the diner and never has a day off."

"Hmm. Sound like someone else you know?" Angus gave her a pointed look and let the door to the diner close.

"I have to provide for my son and my employees."

"Never hurts to ask for help."

"Who would I ask?"

"For now, you have me. You don't have to do it all."

"Well, it will take both of us working until well after dark to get through all the work that needs doing and to take care of the animals. Let's get Tad and head out to Chase's ranch for a few minutes."

Angus nodded. "You're driving."

"Damn right, I am."

"It will be interesting to see if anyone else is experiencing the same level of dangerous accidents."

"Yeah, or if I'm the only target. I need to bump up my life insurance."

Angus braced a hand against the small of her back and guided her to the truck, opened the door and handed her up into it. "Don't start the eulogy yet. You still have me, CW and Jo with our loaded shotguns surrounding you on all sides."

She smiled. "Thanks. I don't know how I'd manage without all of you."

Angus stared at her for a long moment, standing in the doorway, almost touching her. If she wanted to, she could lean out and steal a kiss. If their lovemaking hadn't been a mistake.

God, she was beginning to hate that word and wished she'd never thought of using it in conjunction with the magic she'd shared with Angus.

Angus reached out and cupped her face. "What gets me is that you even have to deal with all of this."

Reggie's heart stopped beating and her breath caught and held for the moment he touched her and looked deep into her eyes.

Then his hand fell to his side and he stepped away, walking around the front of the pickup to climb into the passenger seat.

When she could finally breathe again, Reggie backed out of the parking space and drove the short distance to the school.

Tad's happy face reminded her of what was important. Her son. Not her burgeoning feelings for a cowboy who'd seemingly appeared out of nowhere and could just as easily disappear.

Chapter Thirteen

As soon as Tad climbed into the backseat and Angus buckled him in, the questions started.

"How many snowflakes does it take to fill a bathtub? Wouldn't it be cool to take a bath in snow? How old is Ranger? Is he ever going to get married and have puppies?"

Angus laughed. "Don't you ever breathe?"

"All the time," Tad answered right back. "Are we going to the diner for dinner?"

"Not tonight." Reggie shot a glance in the mirror. "We need to make a stop at the Lucky Lady Ranch to see Mr. Marsden."

"Oh, boy!" Tad bounced in his seat. "Can I pet his bear?"

Angus glanced at Reggie. "This man has a bear? Isn't that dangerous?"

Reggie chuckled. "Only if it was alive. Chase, like me, inherited his ranch. Only he inherited his from his great-grandfather, who was the son of Lady Jones, a locally famous madam who provided services to the miners and ran a gambling hall."

"Interesting family tree."

"Very." Reggie glanced across at Angus.

Angus had the sudden desire to punch a man he'd never met. "How well do you know this Chase?" he asked.

"He's more an acquaintance, since he didn't grow up here. I knew his great-grandfather before he died at the ripe old age of ninety-seven."

"And he worked his ranch up until he died?"

She nodded. "With help. Old Man Marsden loved talking about his grandmother and how she'd won the original property, a mine claim, in a poker game. She was a shrewd businesswoman and put her winnings to work. Within weeks she had miners working the claim. They found a pretty healthy gold vein and milked it for all it would produce. She gave up prostitution, bought up the land around the mine and named the ranch after the mine."

"Wow, talk about winning the lottery."

"Legend had it, she was after the mother lode. When she still owned the gambling hall, before she struck it rich, an old miner would show up once a week with a nugget of gold to pay for a bath, a meal, her services and a bottle of whiskey."

"That's a lot of gold for just those things."

"That's what she thought. When she asked where he got the gold, he said up in the hills between the camel's humps. No one could quite figure out where that was and the old man eventually stopped coming."

"Anyone ever find the camel's humps?"

Reggie shook her head. "Some people think it was on the property I own. The Last Chance Mine was Lady's last-ditch effort to find the mother lode."

"I take it Lady never found it."

Reggie shook her head. "No, and she spent a fortune looking. Finally she gave up and married a railroad tycoon who was also a big-game hunter with a collection of large stuffed animals. Including a thirteen-foot-tall grizzly bear. Chase's great-grandfather sold off the Last Chance Ranch to Ted's grandfather fifty years ago, and Chase inherited the Lucky Lady, the mansion and the collection of trophy carcasses."

Angus grinned. "I was wondering when we'd get to the bear."

"It's ginormous!" Tad exclaimed from the backseat.

Thirty minutes later they arrived in front of a large Colonial-style home that probably dated all the way back to the late eighteen hundreds.

A huge black-and-brown St. Bernard lumbered up to the truck, barking, its paws buried in two inches of snow.

Reggie got out and bent to pet the big animal. "Hey, Barkley."

Tad scrambled down from the backseat and dropped to the ground. "Barkley!"

The dog moved from Reggie to Tad and bowled the child over.

Tad laughed, got back on his feet and hugged the dog.

"I take it you two know each other." Angus chuckled, standing at the front of the truck.

"Tad and Barkley are old friends. Whenever Tad gets lonely for someone to play with, he's welcome to come to the Lucky Lady and play with Barkley."

"How did Tad and Barkley become old friends? The Lucky Lady Ranch is quite a hoof for a five-year-old."

"They met in town last summer. Chase invited Tad out to play with Barkley. He likes that Tad will throw Barkley's ball over and over without getting tired of the game. Tad gets to play. Barkley gets exercise. It's a win-win situation for them both."

"Reggie, sweetheart!" Chase Marsden emerged through the tall, elegant double doors of the big house.

Beside Reggie, Angus tensed. "Seriously? He's your neighbor?"

A thrill of satisfaction rippled through her. Chase Marsden, like his great-great-great-grandmother, was extremely gifted by a squared jaw, smoldering gray-blue eyes and pitch-black hair.

He could easily have stepped onto a model runway at a moment's notice, having all the features any red-blooded woman would find alluring.

"You two are just friends, right?" Angus grumbled.

Reggie chuckled. "Just friends." She reached out to her friend to shake his hand.

He shook her hand, smiling. "How's my favorite neighbor?"

"Fine," Reggie said. "And I'm practically your only neighbor."

The man swept his arm to the side. "Come in, come in." Chase pushed open the front door and stepped back so that Reggie and Angus could enter.

Before they took one step forward, Barkley made a dash through the entrance, Tad following close behind. "Wait for me!"

"Can I get you something to drink? Water, tea or something with a little more kick?" He turned to the bar in the corner of the living room. It could have been a bar straight out of the Old West, with rich wood paneling and backed with a beautifully beveled mirror.

"We really can't stay long. I believe the Christmas pageant is tonight in town, and I promised to take Tad later."

"That should be fun for the little guy." Chase dropped cubes of ice into a crystal glass and poured sparkling water from a bottle over the top of the ice. "Tad, would you like some of that water that tickles your nose?"

"Yes, please!" Tad ran to Chase and Barkley followed, skidding to a stop on the wood floor.

Tad sipped the water from the glass and giggled. "It tickles."

"Does it every time." Chase glanced at Reggie and Angus. "You should come visit when you can stay longer. Barkley could use some exercise and I get bored out here with no one to talk to."

Reggie wished she could stay, but she was always in a hurry with so many chores to deal with on the ranch. Chase seemed like a nice man. Some called him an eccentric billionaire. Reggie just thought he was lonely. "We'd like that another time. Right now we need to know if you've been experiencing any issues with people coming on your property causing trouble?"

"Trouble." Chase frowned. "What kind of trouble?"

"Loosening hinges on gates, leaving fake snakes in places that could spook a horse."

Angus added, "Hitting you or any of your staff in the head with a two-by-four."

Chase's eyes widened. "Reggie? What the hell's been going on at the Last Chance?"

"I don't know. That's what I'm trying to find out."

Angus asked, "Have the mining speculators been out?"

Chase snorted. "Several times. Persistent bastards. And that real estate agent...what's her name?" His brows pulled together.

"Lillian Kuntz?" Reggie offered.

"That's her. Pretty thing." His lips twisted. "Not my type." He glanced up at a framed picture on the wall. "She seemed really interested in my great-great-great-grandmother. Asked all kinds of questions about the history of Fool's Fortune and the Lucky Lady Mine." He pointed at the picture on the wall. "She even asked if I'd sell this map my great-great-great-grandmother had framed."

Angus stepped up beside Chase. "Why would she want it?"

Chase's lips twisted. "It's the map Lady used in her search for the mother lode. Some old customer of hers claimed he'd found it. Brought a chunk of gold in every time he came to town. But he disappeared before anyone could find out where he got it."

Reggie laughed. "I was telling Angus about the legend of the camel's humps on our way out here."

"Lady was obsessed with that mine. She was getting plenty of gold out of the Lucky Lady Mine, but she wanted more."

"There's an X on the map," Angus noted. "Was that supposed to be the location of the old man's mine?"

"Supposedly." Chase lifted his glass to his lips. "I think someone drew up the map and played on my great-great-great-grandmother's greed. No one has ever found that mine. The Last Chance Mine was supposedly where the X fell on the map."

"Do you mind if I take a photo of this map?" Angus asked. He pulled his mobile phone from his pocket.

"Not at all. It's kind of a conversation piece in this house. When the speculator, Vance Peterson, came out, he was interested in the old stories and the map. I guess word got out that Lady was on to something. Seems like everyone's still searching for their pot of gold."

"Not you?" Reggie asked.

"I made my pot of gold in the stock market. I don't need to run after every rumor about a gold mine. I leave that to the zealots with gold fever. I like to control what I have. All that speculating and digging for nothing seems like a waste of time."

"Isn't the stock market a form of speculating?" Angus asked.

"For some." Chase sipped the amber liquid and smiled. "I seem to have a knack for predicting the rise and fall in prices."

Angus aimed his cell phone at the map and snapped a picture.

Reggie watched as he pressed his thumbs to the screen and a whooshing sound followed.

With a nod at the phone, Angus glanced up. "Has anyone been trespassing on your property lately?"

Chase's eyes narrowed and he stared off into a corner. "Last time I rode my ATV up into the hills, I noticed there had been someone poking around the old mines. Not that they'll find anything. Lady did her best to strip all the gold she could find out of them back in her day."

"How do you know someone's been poking around the mines?" Angus asked.

"I found footprints, ATV tracks and evidence of fairly fresh campfires. Could be some kids. In which case, I hope they don't fall down a shaft."

A shiver rippled across Reggie's skin. "It's not hard to slip down one of those shafts. As dark as those mines are, you don't see the shaft until you're on that slippery gravel and shale. I almost fell down one myself before I had Tad." She glanced at her son. Would he be that curious about the old mines when he grew old enough to ride four-wheelers up into the hills?

"The old mines are dangerous," Chase agreed. "Sometimes I think I should seal the entrances. You know, set off an explosion to make the tunnels collapse."

"With an increase in trespassers on your property, have you had any of them try to attack you?" Angus tucked his phone into his pocket.

Chase raised his hands, palms up. "No. Things might actually get interesting if someone did."

Reggie laughed. "Trust me, I could do with a little less excitement around my place."

"I'm sorry, Reggie." Chase set his glass on a table. "Do you want me to send over some of my ranch hands for a week or two until things settle down?"

"Thanks, Chase, but I can manage on my own. I have CW."

"That ol' geezer?" Chase shook his head. "When is he going to retire?"

Reggie smiled. "Never. The ranch is his reason to live. I can't begin to picture him and Jo sitting on a beach in Florida, sipping mai tais." With a glance toward Angus, Reggie said, "I guess we'd better get back to the ranch and get ready for the pageant."

Chase laid a hand on her arm. "Seriously, Reggie, if you're having trouble, let me help. That's what neighbors are for."

She laid a hand over his. "Thanks. I might take you up on that. For now, with CW and Angus, I'm okay."

"Do you have the sheriff involved?" Chase persisted.

"I do." Reggie held out a hand to Tad. "Come on, buddy, it's time to say goodbye to Barkley."

She gave Chase one last look. "You should come to the pageant."

He shrugged. "I'm not much on social gatherings."

"If you change your mind, we'd love to have you along with us. Wouldn't we, Tad?"

Tad's eyes lit. "You could bring Barkley."

Chase shook his head. "Barkley would do what Barkley does best and bark the entire time. The dog has no manners."

Reggie held Tad's hand as they walked toward the door. "If you hear or see anything suspicious—"

"You'll be the first to know." Chase opened the door for them. "Be careful. You're the only neighbor I talk to."

"Thanks for the information. I promise to bring Tad out to visit soon. He's been asking about a puppy lately and I'm too busy right now to take care of one."

"I'll take care of the puppy," Tad said.

"I know, dear." Reggie patted her son's head. "When you're a little bit older."

Reggie thanked Chase, helped Tad into the backseat and climbed behind the steering wheel of her truck.

Angus slid in beside her on the seat, his gaze on the big house and the man standing in the doorway. He hadn't said much during the visit and Reggie wondered what he was thinking. She backed around then shifted into Drive.

"Chase Marsden," Angus mused. "I thought I recognized that name. Isn't he the billionaire who'd been in a race car accident?"

Reggie smiled. "Yeah. He was pretty banged up. He's become somewhat of a recluse since."

"How close *are* you two?"

Reggie's heart fluttered at the question. "We're friends. Nothing else."

"Well, one thing is becoming more clear from that visit."

"Yeah. And what's that?" Reggie asked.

"The attacks are definitely targeting you and the Last Chance Ranch."

AFTER THE VISIT to the Lucky Lady Ranch, Angus didn't feel any better about the situation at the Last Chance Ranch. Whoever was targeting Reggie was making it personal. The steady progression of what looked like accidents to increasingly dangerous attacks had him worried for Reggie and Tad's safety.

"What were you doing with the picture of the map?" Reggie asked.

With a glance in her direction, Angus responded. "I have a friend who works with computers and mapping. Maybe he can figure out if this map is real or just a hoax."

"I don't know why you're bothering. If Lady

couldn't find the mother lode mine with that map, it can't be found. At least not with the map. She was one very determined woman."

"If someone thinks the map is the key to finding gold on your ranch, they might be willing to do anything to get to it."

Reggie didn't respond. When she pulled up beside the house, Jo came out on the porch, wringing her hands.

Angus and Reggie dropped down out of the truck.

"What's wrong, Mrs. Reinhardt?" Angus asked.

"Thank goodness you're home." Jo wrung her hands, glancing toward the barn. "Somehow the gate to the pasture was left open. The cattle and the horses have disappeared out of the lower pens to who knows where. CW is saddling up now to go find them."

Reggie frowned. "CW doesn't need to be chasing after the herd."

"I told him that, but he didn't want to wait until sunset to go out looking for them. If you hurry, you might catch him before he gets away. He was headed for the barn the last time I spoke with him."

"We'll catch him," Angus assured the woman.

Tad climbed down from the truck. "I guess we're not going to the Christmas pageant?"

"Oh, Tad, I'm sorry." Reggie dropped to her haunches in front of her son. "Maybe next year."

"Tad—" Jo touched the boy's shoulder "—if they catch Mr. Reinhardt before he gets out of the barnyard, he and I will take you to the Christmas pageant."

"Really?" Tad's face brightened.

"Yes, sir. I was going to go before Mr. Reinhardt decided to chase after livestock."

"You don't mind?" Reggie asked. "Don't feel like you have to. Tad will get over it."

"Not at all." Jo waved a hand. "CW and I had planned on going until the animals got out. Though we'll have to leave early enough to beat the weather home. Weatherman is calling for more snow late tonight."

"We'd better hurry before CW gets too far," Angus said. "Reggie and I will get the animals back before dark." He hurried around the side of the house toward the barn.

The barn door opened and CW led out the horse Angus had ridden the day before. A long rope hung from the saddle as well as a rifle scabbard, with a rifle in it.

When CW spotted Angus, he hurried forward. "Oh, good. I could use your help. The horses and cattle are out. Somehow the gate got left open this afternoon and all the animals got loose. I was working in the barn all afternoon and didn't notice until they'd made their escape. They're probably headed up into the hills."

"Don't worry. Reggie and I will bring them back."

"No use in Ms. Reggie going. I'm all saddled up and ready. Besides, you two just got back from being out all night."

"We're fine." Angus grabbed the horse's bridle. "Besides, Mrs. Jo and Tad had their hearts set on going to the Christmas pageant tonight. They're waiting on you."

CW frowned. "I'd rather go after the animals."

"Reggie would feel better knowing you were doing the driving. The roads are slick with the recent snow and ice."

"Still would rather have a root canal than go to the pageant."

"Mr. CW," Tad called out, running toward them. "Mrs. Jo said you'd take us to the Christmas pageant if Angus caught you before you left to find the cows."

Reggie followed Tad around the side of the house. "Angus and I will stay behind and bring the animals home. I'd wait until tomorrow and come with you now, but we're supposed to get more snow tonight."

"Three hands are better than two," CW argued.

"I know, but Mrs. Jo promised Tad she'd take him to town for the pageant. I'd feel better knowing they had you to look out for them." She touched CW's arm.

Tad smiled up at CW and held out his hand. "Come on. We have to hurry or we'll miss the parade."

CW walked with the boy back to the house.

"I'll get my horse," Reggie, said.

While she saddled her gelding, Angus led his horse to the gate that opened toward the hill where the cattle and horses had disappeared. He unlatched the gate, led his horse through and waited for Reggie.

She emerged from the barn moments later with her gelding.

Angus closed the gate behind Reggie and mounted his horse, tucking his prosthetic foot into the stirrup.

Reggie placed her foot in the stirrup and gracefully swung up into the saddle. "Ready?"

The light snow dusting the ground from the night before made the tracks easy to follow, leading back the way he and Reggie had come that morning. The farther away from the house and barn they got, the more concerned Angus became.

Reggie stopped beside a muddy set of tracks at the base of the hill leading up over the top of the dangerous ridge. She glanced down at a mix of snow, mud, hoof prints and tire tracks. "ATV."

Angus had seen them. "Driving the animals away from the house and barn."

"Why?"

His gut knotted. "My bet is that whoever is driving the herd is setting you up for another attack."

Reggie stared off in the direction of the animal and ATV tracks. "I can't leave the horses and cattle out here. If the weather gets too bad, they could be trapped in an upper meadow. I won't be able to get hay to them."

If he didn't have the rifle with them, Angus would have insisted they return to the house for arms. "I'd feel better if you went back to the house and let me handle this."

Even before he finished speaking, she was shaking her head. "It's my ranch. I have to be able to take care of the animals and deal with trespassers, otherwise whoever is attacking me might consider me weak."

"Being cautious isn't the same as being weak."

She snorted. "Maybe to you. But the men in this line of work see females as less than capable of taking care of a ranch this size. I have to work twice as hard to earn their respect." Sitting tall in the saddle, her cheeks pink from the cool, crisp air, Reggie looked tough, determined and even more desirable as a woman.

Angus's hands tightened on his reins. *How'd she do that?* "I don't want this to come off as a reflection of the job you're doing running the ranch, but, please, at least let me lead the way."

Reggie sucked in a deep breath and let it out on a puff of vapor in the cold air. "Okay."

Angus clucked his tongue and said, "Get up." He didn't have to nudge the horse. That simple word set the horse in motion.

Passing Reggie and her horse, Angus continued up the trail along the side of the hill to the steep ridge. As he crested the ridge, the sun chose that moment to peek from behind clouds, blinding him.

A sudden revving of a motor alerted him to trouble right before a four-wheeler barreled up over the top of the hill, heading straight for him.

Angus's horse reared and danced to the side of the trail, kicking rocks and gravel over the edge of a three-hundred-foot, almost vertical drop.

The ATV blasted past Angus and nearly ran into Reggie and her horse.

When Angus's horse dropped back on all fours and got its hooves firmly on the trail, Angus grabbed the rope from the side of his saddle. He would have gone after the ATV and rider if Reggie and her horse weren't blocking the path. Her gelding reared, nearly unseating her, its back hooves shifting perilously close to the edge.

When she had the horse steady, she glanced over her shoulder.

The ATV had raced down the hill, turned and was headed back at them.

"Get out of the way!" Angus shouted, urging his mare past the gelding on the drop-off side of the trail. Angus charged down the hill toward their attacker.

The rider slowed and turned around, the trail barely wide enough for him to turn. He had to rock the ATV back and forth until he got it all the way around. By that time, Angus had caught up to him.

With his rope in one hand, the reins in the other, Angus lifted his arm, praying his days of junior rodeo would come back to him. He flung the rope, caught the rider in the loop and yanked him out of his seat and onto the ground.

Without its rider, the ATV rolled to a stop against the face of a rocky cliff.

The rider staggered to his feet and struggled to free himself from the rope.

Angus backed his horse, tightening the line on his captive.

"Let me go!" the man yelled.

Angus tied the rope to the saddle horn, pulled his foot out of the stirrup and slid to the ground.

The horse did its job, backing up to keep the rope tight.

Angus hurried toward the rider and reached for the buckle of the man's helmet, freeing the strap. He pulled the helmet off the attacker's head. A man with dirty, light brown hair, glared at him.

Behind Angus, Reggie gasped. "Daniel Freeman."

The survivalist Mr. Cramer had mentioned in town.

Angus grabbed the man by the collar of his jacket and lifted him half off the ground. "Why were you trying to run us over?"

"I wasn't trying to run you over. I was just trying to get down the trail."

"Yeah." Angus lifted him higher. "I might have bought that but you turned around to do it again. Too bad you got caught."

"Why are you driving my herd up into the hills?" Reggie demanded.

Freeman's lips clamped shut and he didn't answer.

"I suggest you answer the lady before we call the cops and have you arrested for attempted murder," Angus warned.

The man stared at Angus for a moment before saying, "I was paid to move the cattle."

"Paid?" Reggie shook her head. "By who?"

Freeman sneered. "Someone who gave me a lot of money to keep that information to myself."

"Did the same person pay you to hit Ms. Davis in the head with a two-by-four?"

The man blinked. "I don't know nuthin' about hitting Ms. Davis."

"What about the fake snake?" Reggie asked.

Freeman snorted. "Got paid good for that, too."

"And the loose hinges?" Reggie demanded.

"Guilty. But if you take me to court it'll be my word against yours. And you'd have to catch me first."

Angus raised the man by his collar until his feet dangled off the ground. "Seems I've already caught you."

The man's face turned a deep red, his eyes bulging.

"Why are you trying to kill me?" Reggie asked.

"I'm not." Freeman coughed, obviously choking. "I was paid to use scare tactics. That's all."

"Who paid you?" Angus repeated, raising him higher, his arms straining.

"Can't...say," the man rasped, his voice pinched.

Reggie touched his arm. "Put him down, Angus. You can't kill him."

Angus hesitated for a long moment and then slowly lowered the man until his feet were firmly on the ground. He released him and stepped back.

A little too late, Angus realized the horse had shifted, relaxing the tension on the rope.

Freeman shimmied out of the lasso, bent at the waist and plowed into Angus's gut.

Angus crashed into Reggie before he hit the ground on his backside.

Reggie screamed, her arms flailing as she fell backward over the edge of the cliff.

Unable to turn fast enough to catch her, all Angus could do was watch as she slid down the extremely steep drop-off until she disappeared past an outcropping of rocks.

While Angus scrambled to get his fake leg beneath him and rise, Freeman ran to his ATV. He mounted, revved the engine and raced down the hill, out of range of the rifle in the scabbard on the side of Angus's saddle.

Angus didn't give a damn about Freeman. His heart in his throat, he low-crawled to the edge of the trail and peered over the side. "Reggie!" he cried. His breath caught and held. Please be okay. After a long moment, he heard her faint reply.

"Angus. Help me."

Chapter Fourteen

Reggie clung to a scraggly pine tree wedged into the side of the cliff. Its roots tangled around the rocks, their tentative grasp on the sheer rock face the only thing holding the tree and her from plummeting the remaining two hundred and eighty feet to their deaths.

Her heart banged against her ribs as she strained the muscles in her arms to hang on.

"Regina?" Angus called out.

"Down here."

"How far?"

"I think about twenty feet from the top. Just under a rocky outcropping."

"Hang on. I'm coming."

She let out a breathy laugh, the sound more of a sob. "I'm hanging." Reggie didn't dare glance down. If the roots broke loose of the rocks, she'd see the bottom soon enough.

She shivered; glad for her coat and the gloves she'd worn that day. Dangling by a tree branch, the cold December wind blasting through the mountains seemed even colder than before. "Are you going to send for help?"

"Only if I have to," he responded.

Reggie wished she could see his face. The rocky outcropping kept her from seeing the trail above.

Something popped and the tree branch lurched. "If you could hurry, I'd be ever so grateful."

"Coming."

A rope dropped down near to where she clung to the scraggly tree. It dangled like a carrot in front of a donkey. Too far away, even if she could let go of the tree with one hand to reach for it.

"I see your rope," she called. She braced one arm around the tiny tree and reached out. The tree quivered and she grabbed hold of it with both hands again, her eyes burning with unshed tears. "I can't reach it."

"Don't try. I'm coming down to get you."

"No. It's too dangerous. Go back to the ranch house and call for help."

"I can't leave you out here that long." Gravel rained down on her. "I won't leave you," he added softly.

She heard and her chest tightened. "I don't want you to risk it. It's a three-hundred-foot drop to the bottom."

"I can see that." More gravel dropped down on

her. Reggie closed her eyes and prayed the tree would remain firmly fixed to the cliff.

A scraping sound near her made her open her eyes.

Angus had rappelled down the cliff, the rope twisted through a D-ring and a makeshift rope harness seat. With one hand behind him holding the line and slowing his descent, he came to a stop three feet to her right. "Hey, darlin'."

"How did you do that?" She stared up the rope toward the top.

In a sitting position, he walked sideways toward her, holding the downhill portion of the rope in the small of his back. "Don't move."

"Trust me. I won't. It's the tree I'm worried about." Her muscles burned from the strain of holding on.

"I'm going to drop a little lower and slide in behind you."

"Just don't bump me. My branch is barely strong enough to hold me."

"I'll be careful." He eased to the side, lowering himself just enough to come up behind her. He stepped around her and cupped her with his body, his legs on either side of hers.

Reggie's body shook. One bad bump and the little tree would break loose. She wanted to lean back into the warmth of Angus's body, but didn't dare.

"I've got my feet braced against the cliff.

You're going to have to let go of the tree and grab hold of me." He spoke softly, his tone calm, matter-of-fact.

She didn't want to let go of the tree. For the past few minutes it was the only thing between her and the bottom of the cliff. "I can't."

"Give me your hand." His voice firm, he talked to her. "Just one hand."

Taking a deep breath, she held it and reached out to take his hand.

"I need you to turn and wrap your legs around me."

"Nope. Not happening," she said, holding on to the tree with one arm while squeezing his hand, his grip reassuring.

"Come on, I know you're tougher than that. You're a one-woman ranch owner, determined to make this ranch work."

"I'm tired. I can't do this anymore."

"Sure you can. You have a terrific kid who needs you." Angus tugged her hand, gently guiding her to him. "All you have to do is wrap your arms around me and hold on. Think of it as a great big hug. Come on. I know you've been wanting to."

Despite the desperate fear of falling to her death, Reggie couldn't resist the warmth of Angus's voice. God, she wanted to hug him right then, and hold on to him for dear life.

He placed the hand he held around his waist. "That's it. Now the other."

"I can't," she whispered, but she gripped his belt, and hung on, transferring her weight to him. Then she let go and grabbed with the other hand, locking her arms around his middle.

For a moment the rope swung out, twisting in the air.

Then Angus planted his legs on either side of her and his heels dug into the cliff.

"Now what?" Reggie asked.

He tied the end of the rope around them both. "Just hang on and let me worry about that." He clucked his tongue and spoke in a firm voice that carried up to the top of the cliff. "Get up."

A faint nickering sounded, but nothing happened.

"Come on, girl. Get up," he repeated with a little more oomph this time.

The rope jerked.

Reggie clung to Angus, burying her face in his belly. "You have a horse pulling us up?"

"That's the plan." He clucked his tongue. "Get up."

The rope stretched taut with the weight of both of them. Then they moved, slowly rising up the face of the cliff. Angus held on to her while walking his feet up the sheer rock wall.

"As we near the top, it'll get a little trickier," Angus said.

She snorted, trying hard not to sob. "And what we just did wasn't tricky?" Reggie glanced up as they neared the trail above. The rope scraped the edge, dragging through the gravel.

"Whoa," Angus called out.

When their heads were three feet from the edge, they stopped.

Angus glanced down into her eyes. "I need you to climb up onto my legs, turn around, grab the ledge and let me push you up over the top."

She shook her head, her arms tightening around his middle. "If that means letting go of you... I don't know."

"I'll hold on to you," he assured her.

Her arms shook as she released her hold around his waist and levered herself up on his legs.

Angus looped his arms around her waist and helped until she got her knees up on his thighs. With her hands braced on his shoulders, she placed one foot, then the other on his legs and stood.

"Turn around and hold on to the rope. When you're ready, pull yourself up. I'll push from behind." Every word Angus spoke was deep, calm and steady.

Reggie needed that steady tone when her entire body shook. She turned, placing her feet carefully on his thighs, praying his prosthetic was strapped on tightly. As soon as she could see the rope, she reached for it and held on.

"Now, brace your hands on the ledge and pull yourself up."

"I don't know if I have the upper body strength."

"I'll be pushing from behind. Just do it," Angus said through gritted teeth. "I don't know how long the horse will stay put. And I hate to point it out, but the rope is fraying."

"Going." Afraid for him as much as for herself, she placed her hands on the edge and pushed up until her belly pressed into the rocky ledge. As she pulled her leg up over the side, she swayed and almost fell backward. She steadied herself, her heart hammering against her ribs.

A hand planted firmly on her derriere gave her a healthy shove, sending her flying face-first onto the gravel trail.

For a moment she lay spread-eagle, hugging the earth, thankful for arriving safe after clinging to her life on nothing more than a scraggly tree.

Angus's mare pawed at the ground, whinnied and backed up a step. The rope scraped against the sharp ledge, strands popping with the strain and friction.

The top of Angus's head disappeared.

No. Her pulse pounding, her breath caught in

her throat, Reggie low-crawled toward the side of the cliff. "Hold on, Angus."

"I'm holding, but that rope isn't going to make it much longer."

Reggie eased back from the edge. Once she was sure she wouldn't fall over the side, she shot to her feet. Crossing to the mare, she gathered her reins and led her away from Angus, glancing over her shoulder to ensure the man made it to the top.

When he appeared again, she let go of the breath she'd been holding.

"Keep going," Angus called. "Hurry!"

The rope jerked as another strand broke.

The mare strained against the weight and drag on her. She tossed her head and whinnied.

"It's okay, just a little farther," Reggie coaxed the animal, speaking softly when she wanted to yell and scream to get moving.

Angus slowly eased up to the top of the ledge. When he was close enough, he pushed up and flung his legs over the side.

Still moving forward and with less resistance, the mare dragged Angus along the gravel a few feet before Reggie could get her to stop.

"Whoa." Reggie moved in front of the mare and held tightly to her bridle. "It's okay. You did it." She smoothed a hand over the mare's nose. With a calming hand sliding along the animal's neck, Reggie walked around to her side and worked the knot loose from the saddle horn, releasing the rope.

Then she ran to where Angus lay on the ground.

He rolled over and lay on his back, staring up at the sky.

Reggie dropped to her knees beside him. "Are you okay?" She cupped his face and brushed a hand across his forehead. "Holy hell. I didn't think we were going to make it."

He raised his hand to her cheek and smiled. "Failure wasn't an option."

Her heart rate having begun to slow, sped away at the look in Angus's eyes. "I almost lost it when the horse backed up and you disappeared." She bent and swept her lips across his. "And the rope was fraying…" She touched her lips to his again. "And the horse was getting antsy…"

This time when her lips met his, Angus's hands circled the back of her neck. "We're both safe now. Everything is going to be okay." Then he kissed her, his mouth moving over hers, his tongue skimming the seam of her lips until she parted them on a sigh.

When his tongue slid along hers, she melted into him, her breasts pressing against his chest. Heat suffused her body, chasing out the cold dread of falling over the cliff and clinging to life on a tree branch.

She finally broke the kiss to breathe and she

pressed her forehead to his. "Thank you for saving my life. I don't know how much longer I could have held on." She laughed, her heart lighter. "I don't know how much longer that tree's roots could have held on. And thank you for not leaving me to get help."

"I couldn't." His arms tightened around her. "The thought of you not being there when I got back made me do what I had to do. Here. Now." He sat up, pulling her across his lap.

Snow drifted down, spotting his hair with lacy flakes. Reggie sighed. "We still have horses and cattle to get down out of the hills and it's getting dark, not to mention a mercenary bastard to catch."

"Right." Angus's lips twisted. "Nothing like a near-death experience to remind us that we're alive and still have work to do."

Reggie kissed him again and stood then reached out her hand to help him up.

ANGUS TOOK HER hand and let her help him to his feet. His good leg shook with the residual nerves of almost crashing to the bottom of the cliff. He was glad for her hand and held on longer than necessary. Once he was upright and steady, he pulled her into his arms and hugged her close.

"You scared the hell out of me."

"I scared you?" She laughed. "Come on, let's not dwell on it."

"You're right." He set her away from him and eased her back from the edge of the trail. "But if it's all the same to you, I'd rather you didn't mount up until we get past this drop-off."

Reggie stared at the place she'd gone over the edge. "Agreed." She gathered her gelding's reins and led him farther along the trail.

Angus followed with his mare.

The path leveled and opened out into a gently sloping meadow where the missing horses and cattle grazed on the grass beneath a light dusting of snow.

Reggie immediately mounted and rode out to the farthest point.

Angus took a few moments longer, swinging up into the saddle and positioning his foot in the stirrup. Soon he was helping round up the herd alongside Reggie.

They worked well together, gathering the stragglers into formation and guiding them to the path leading home. By the time they had the horses and cattle moving in the right direction, the snow had grown heavier and the trail was slippery.

The herd moved slowly, plodding up the narrow path, single-file. Angus held back, glancing back once more to make certain they hadn't left an animal behind.

When he was certain, he fell in behind Reggie, his chest tightening as they moved past the point where she'd fallen over the cliff.

Ranching cattle and horses had its own set of dangers, but in the foothills of the Rocky Mountains there were different challenges. He was beginning to agree with her friends and neighbors. Reggie had too much to handle. She'd already lost her husband to the perilous terrain. Would she continue to push until something happened to her? And what would happen when he left? She'd be on her own. Who would save her if she fell over another cliff?

The uneventful trip back to the ranch gave Angus far too much time to worry over the situation and Reggie. By the time they had the cattle and horses back in the lower pasture and the gates securely closed behind them, darkness had settled over the land. Clouds lowered over the hills, dumping snow so thick, Angus could barely see his hand in front of his face.

He rode his horse up to the barn, swung out of the saddle and dropped to the ground.

Reggie rode up beside him, her face scraped from her fall, snowflakes dusting her shoulders and hair. She smiled down at him. "Thanks. I couldn't have done it without you."

Angus reached up. "Come here."

She let him lift her out of the saddle and she slid down his front, her body flush up against his.

Even bundled in a thick coat and gloves, she felt good in his arms. He pressed a kiss to her lips and set her on the ground.

"I could get used to coming off the trail like that," she whispered. A fat snowflake landed on the tip of her nose.

Angus kissed it off and smiled. "I can take care of the horses. Why don't you go on up to the house?"

She shook her head. "As tired as I am, the horses have to be exhausted, too. I don't rest until my horse is fed and brushed."

He nodded, admiring her determination to take care of her animals before herself. "Fair enough." He opened the barn door for her and waited while she led her gelding in.

He followed and tied his mare to a post.

Within a few short minutes they had the saddles off, horses brushed and feed in the troughs.

A lonely, wailing howl sounded outside the building.

"The storm got here early," Reggie said. About the time she reached for the latch on the barn door, the lights blinked out. "And there goes the electricity. We'd better get back to the house before it gets any worse."

When Reggie opened the door, it was ripped from her hands by the wind.

Angus stepped out, grabbed the door and forced it closed against the wind. In the short time they'd been in the barn, the wind had picked up, blowing the falling snow sideways. Angus couldn't see two feet in front of his face.

Reggie reached out a hand for his. "Stay with me!" she shouted and then leaned into the gale-force winds, her head down, her collar pulled up.

Angus had heard of people getting lost in blizzards when going from their outbuildings to their houses. Though he was familiar with snow and blustery weather, the blinding snow worried him. Not until they reached the back porch did he relax and feel safe.

Reggie pushed through the back door, a blast of wind carrying snow in with her.

Angus entered behind her and shut the door as quickly as he could.

No matter how much his eyes adjusted, Angus could see nothing in the pitch-black of the house.

The sound of a light switch being flicked was followed by a sigh. "So much for electricity. It could be down for a couple days."

"Do you have a flashlight close by?" Angus asked.

"Should be one in the drawer." The sound of a drawer opening and closing was followed by a click. A beam of light cut through the darkness. Reggie smiled. "That's better."

Angus shook off the snow from his hat and jacket and shrugged out of them, hanging them on a hook beside the back door.

Reggie called out, "Tad?" No answer. "CW? Jo?"

Taking the flashlight from Reggie, Angus

helped her out of her coat and hung it on another hook.

Reggie shivered and rubbed her arms. "We'll have to light a fire in the fireplace or it'll get pretty darned cold tonight. Though we have gas heat, the blower won't run without electricity."

"Do you have a gas-powered generator?"

"We do. I had CW check it out a couple of days ago. It's on the back porch."

"I'll take care of it."

"Not now. Wait until we *have* to use it. The house is still relatively warm. The water heaters are gas, so we should be able to get hot showers. Anything in the fridge and freezer can be set out on the porch to keep." She toed her boots off and padded across the kitchen floor in her socks. "First thing, though. I want to know where Tad, Jo and CW are."

"Do you think they got caught in town?"

"Probably. I sure hope they don't try to make it home in this."

Angus followed her into the living room. While Reggie checked phone messages, Angus wandered over to the fireplace. Wood was stacked neatly beside the hearth and the fireplace was clean and empty. Checking the flue functionality, he left it open and then built a small stack of kindling and newspaper, lit the paper and waited until the kindling burned. Once the flames took off, he added logs to the stack. Soon a cheerful fire crackled, providing both warmth and light in the room.

Reggie pressed a button on the voice-mail recorder.

"Ms. Reggie, it's Jo. The weather started getting bad while we were eating at the diner. Kitty offered to put us up until the bad stuff blows over. Looks like we'll be staying the night. Tad's fine. He's excited to get to stay at Ms. Kitty's. She put him to work rolling utensils for her customers. Call us and let us know you and Angus are okay. We hate to think of you two out in the storm. Well, okay, talk to you soon."

"Thank God." Reggie lifted the receiver and pressed it to her ear. "No signal. The phone lines must be down too, and cell phones don't get much reception this far out. I hate for them to worry, but there's no way to let them know we're okay."

"You can't run into town any more than they can get out to us."

Reggie sighed. "You're right."

"It also means we won't be able to call the sheriff and report Daniel Freeman's part in the attacks on you. He could be in the next state by the time the sheriff can do anything about it."

"If he's caught in this storm, he won't get very far." Reggie shoved her hand through her hair. "I guess it's just you and me tonight."

Chapter Fifteen

The hungry gleam in Angus's eyes made Reggie's pulse race. "I've got a couple of sleeping bags in the linen closet. If we plan on staying warm tonight, it'll be here in the living room by the fire." With the flashlight in hand, she practically ran from the room back to the kitchen.

Reggie dug five candles out of a cabinet, lit one, left it on the kitchen counter and carried the other candles with her into the living room. She lit two there and moved on to the bedroom Angus was using. The room was clean, the bed neatly made and Ranger lay on his dog bed, giving her a sad look. She opened the door wider and the dog rose, sniffed her hand and licked it as if to thank her. Then he trotted out of the bedroom and down the hallway to the living room.

In the master bathroom she lit the last candle and set it on the edge of the big bathtub. The orange glow surrounded the tub in flickering romantic light.

Reggie's breath caught and she pressed her hand against her breasts. What would it be like to climb in that tub with Angus, to stretch out naked in steaming water? Her nipples tightened and an ache burned low in her body.

Was a year long enough to grieve for the husband she'd lost? Making love to Angus in the mine had seemed so natural. Was it wrong of her to want to make love to another man in the same house she'd shared with Ted? The house Ted's great-grandfather had built and passed down to his son and his son's son?

After more than a year without her husband, Reggie craved a man's touch. But not any man. She craved Angus's hands on her body. She wanted to lie next to him, skin-to-skin, holding each other throughout the night.

Even more she wanted that empty space inside her filled. The only man who'd sparked her interest and lit a fire deep in her soul was Angus. Heat rose up her chest and neck into her cheeks.

She twisted the handle on the water, tested the temperature and headed for the linen closet where she stored the sleeping bags.

When she reentered the living room, she carried two rolled sleeping bags and tossed them on the couch. Ranger lay on the rug in front of the fireplace, happily warming himself. Angus was nowhere to be seen.

Good. She wouldn't be tempted to invite

Angus to join her in the bath that was quickly filling. She could lie in the warm water all by herself, imagining what it would be like to be with him, and tell herself it was the right thing to keep a physical distance from the man.

Then why were her nerves strung tight and the hunger inside building to an incredible ache that couldn't be assuaged by her imagination?

It's for the best. Telling herself she was relieved, she marched down the hall toward her bedroom where she'd take a quiet bath. Alone.

As she came abreast of Angus's room, he stepped out, wearing nothing but his jeans.

So intent on making it to her room, Reggie barely stopped before plowing into him. Though she had every intention of keeping her hands off Angus, she must have leaned toward him.

He reached out, his arms wrapping around her waist, pulling her against his naked chest.

Reggie rested her palms on the hard plane of muscles, her breath stolen from her lungs. Slowly she glanced up, her gaze rising from her hands up his bulky chest and neck to his lips. There she stopped, her tongue wiping across her own dry mouth. "I..." she squeaked, cleared her throat and tried again. "I was on my way to my room."

He chuckled, the deep tone humming through his chest into hers. "Reggie," he said. "We don't have to make this hard." His hands tightened around her.

"Don't we?" she said, her gaze shifting upward to connect with his.

"We can walk away and forget everything that's happened between us," he assured her, his chest rising and falling beneath her hands.

She shook her head, barely able to concentrate on his words, her fingers curling into his skin. "I think we're past forgetting."

He dragged in a deep breath and let it out slowly, his hungry gaze skimming over her face. "Tell me to let go and I will. Otherwise, I'll keep holding on."

"I can't." She reached up and cupped his face. "I want you. God, I want you more than anything I've ever wanted in my life." There, she'd admitted it to his face. She couldn't take it back, and at that moment she didn't want to.

"I've never wanted a woman more than I want you. Ever." He kissed her softly and raised his head. "Before or after the explosion."

Her eyes stinging with the force of her mixed-up emotions, Reggie leaned up on her toes and kissed him, pressing her lips against his, thrusting her tongue past his teeth to taste his.

His arms tightened, crushing her to his chest, deepening the kiss until she couldn't remember where she ended and he began.

When he finally lifted his head, he pressed his cheek to her temple. "What are we going to do?"

She smiled, her heart leaping. Stepping out

of the circle of his arms, she held out her hand. "Follow me."

Hurrying, before reason or guilt could poison the moment and make her change her mind, she led him down the hall, through the master bedroom and into the bathroom where the big air-jet tub sat, half full of steaming water.

She turned off the faucet.

Angus's gaze swept over the bath and he pulled her around to face him, catching both of her hands in his. "Are you sure?"

Reggie nodded, her gaze steady. "I'm sure." To prove it, she grabbed the hem of her shirt and pulled it up over her head, letting it fall to the floor at her feet. Then she unclipped the back of her bra.

Angus held up his hands. "You realize to get into that bath, I have to take off my prosthetic."

Her eyes widened. "So?"

"You won't be upset?"

"That you have only one leg?" She could tell by the intensity of his gaze that exposing himself—all of him—to her would be a big step for him.

With her gaze locked on his, she let her bra slide down over her arms, dropping it on the floor along with her shirt. Then she reached for the button and zip on his jeans. "I wouldn't have brought you in here if it bothered me." She tipped her head to the side. "From our night in the mine,

I know your injury doesn't impact your…er, other abilities." With a smile, she slid the zipper down. "I'm willing to take the risk. Are you?"

Angus's heart squeezed so hard in his chest, he forgot how to breathe. Since his injury and subsequent therapy, the only people who had seen his stump of a leg had been the doctors, nurses and physical therapist, along with other soldiers in the large therapy rooms where he'd spent much of his time learning how to walk with the prosthetic.

Now, standing in front of Reggie, his member rock-hard and ready, he wanted to shed his insecurities and dive into the tub naked with her. But he couldn't. She needed to be fully aware of who and what he was before she committed to sliding naked into the bathtub with him.

Her hand on his zipper cranked up his internal thermometer, the heat spreading throughout his body.

She pulled it down, her gaze never leaving his. When the zipper was all the way down, his member sprang free into the palm of her hand.

With a smile, she circled her fingers around him and held him firmly.

His breath caught and held. "Last chance to back out. I'll understand."

She shook her head. "I'm not backing out.

Perhaps you are the one who needs the option to back out."

For a moment he considered it, but the warmth in her eyes and the heat in her hand catapulted him over the edge of reason. He shoved his jeans down over his hips.

Reggie released him long enough to join his hand with her own to take the denim all the way to his ankles.

He pulled his leg out of the jeans and paused with his hands on the button to release his prosthetic leg.

Reggie covered her hand with his and he waited. Had she changed her mind?

She pushed his hands aside and worked the straps loose.

Angus slipped his thigh out of the device and set it aside, hopping on his remaining foot. Naked, exposed and more vulnerable than he cared to admit, he gave her the opportunity to back out.

Reggie unbuttoned her jeans, slid the zipper down and then shoved the jeans and her panties down her legs, stepping out of them. She sat on the edge of the bath and swung her legs over the side, sliding down into the water. Once settled, she held out her hand. "Please, join me."

His pulse pounding so hard it reverberated in his ears, Angus lowered himself to the side of the bath and swung his leg over the side. Then he eased into the steaming water, the heat wrapping around him, the candle casting a golden hue over the bath and Reggie.

"You're beautiful," he said as he settled in the tub beside her and pulled her into his arms.

His heart beat so fast, he could barely breathe. Her leg rested against his half leg, the water warm around him, caressing his body much as she was.

"You're not so bad yourself." She slid her hand across his chest, tweaking the little brown nipples. Her fingers ducked beneath the surface of the water, running down over his torso, belly and hip.

His member swelled, throbbing with his need to take this woman and be with her in the most intimate way.

She didn't stop at his hip, reaching lower to the scarred stump. "Can I touch?"

He forced air in and out of his lungs, praying the phantom pain would remain at bay and that Reggie wouldn't be unnerved by his deformity. Finally he nodded.

She touched his leg, her fingers tracing the scars. "Does it still hurt?"

He nodded. "Sometimes. My nerves send pain messages to my brain telling me my calf and foot hurt even though they aren't there."

"It must have been hard adjusting."

"Not as hard as adjusting to the fact my men died that day."

Her hand caressed him fearlessly. "Someday, I hope you'll tell me about it."

His eyes burned and his throat clogged with emotion. He wanted to tell her about the explosion, about the men who'd died and his own wake-up call when the doctor told him he'd lost his leg. Angus hadn't even talked to the shrink about what had happened. But with Reggie, he'd never felt more able to speak freely without censure or pity. "I will. Someday." He captured her hand and brought it up to his chest. "Right now, I can think of better things to do than talk."

Reggie rolled over, braced her hands on either side of him and pressed her breasts against his chest. "And what might that be? Perhaps a kiss?" She brushed her lips across his. "Or did you have something else in mind?" With a wicked smile, she straddled his hips and reached behind him, producing a foil packet from a bowl filled with scented soaps.

His member grew impossibly hard, rising out of the water, throbbing with the need to be buried deep inside this woman who was not only brave and strong but also incredibly resourceful.

She tore the packet open and rolled the protection down over him. Then she raised herself up and eased down, her hand guiding him inside her warm, slick channel.

"You feel so good," he moaned.

"I could say the same." Reggie rose and lowered herself onto him again and again, increasing in speed and intensity. She threw back her head, her eyes squeezing shut, her face tensing.

Angus thrust upward for each time she came down, his body on fire, every nerve ending pulsing with desire. Water splashed around them and onto the floor. Neither cared, so caught up in the moment it didn't matter.

He cupped her breasts, squeezing as she moved. The faster she rocked, the more powerful the sensations, until he shot past any grip he had on control and soared over the edge. As he slowly returned to earth, he captured the back of her neck and pulled her down until he could kiss her, driving his tongue into her mouth, stroking hers. "You're amazing."

She rested against his chest, her soft breasts squashed between them.

The water grew cold as the air temperature dropped in the bathroom.

"We should move to the living room with the fireplace."

Reggie leaned back and shivered. "You're right." Once more she bent to kiss him then rose out of the water and grabbed a towel.

Angus scooted up to the edge of the tub and swung his leg over.

Reggie handed him a towel and he dried off,

then reattached his prosthetic. He pushed to his feet and wrapped the towel around himself.

With her towel wrapped snugly around her body and tucked in at the side of her breast, Reggie looked even more beautiful, more tempting. Her cheeks reddened and her gaze dipped. "We better get some clothes on."

Angus shook his head and closed the widening gap between them. "Let's not make this awkward."

She tipped her head to the side. "Who said anything about being awkward?"

"You looked embarrassed."

Her lips lifted in a smile. "I am, a little. Embarrassed at how much I want to do that again."

Angus scooped her up in his arms.

"Put me down."

"I will." He strode through the door of the bathroom, through the bedroom and down the hallway into the living room where the fire blazed in the fireplace and the air temperature was considerably warmer.

Reggie snuggled in his arms, running a finger over his collarbone. "You know you do that pretty good for a one-legged cowboy."

He stumbled and almost lost his footing. "What did you say?"

She poked his chest. "You heard me."

He shook his head, lowering her legs until her feet touched the ground. "A one-legged cowboy?"

"Does that hurt your feelings?" Reggie chewed her bottom lip. "I'm sorry if it did. Even if it is the truth."

A chuckle rose from his throat, followed by another and another until he was clutching his sides with full belly laughs.

What felt like a huge weight lifted from his shoulders; a heaviness that had been with him since the moment he realized he was no longer whole, faded away as though it had never been.

Reggie, the indomitable woman with attitude, gumption and fearlessness, who'd nearly fallen to her death that same day, had infused hope and optimism in a damaged ex-soldier. She didn't pity him and she sure as hell wasn't going to pussyfoot around his infirmity. She was matter-of-fact and curious.

And beautiful, soft and sensuous. Everything he could ever want in a woman. She loved fiercely and completely, as demonstrated in her love for her son, her love for her dead husband and the people she called family.

"No, it doesn't bother me. And you're right. I am a one-legged cowboy."

Her smile returned. "And you get along better than some two-legged cowboys I've known. And you're much sexier."

He brushed a strand of her sandy-blond hair off her cheek, tucking it behind her ear. "When you say things like that…it makes me want to…"

"Kiss me?" She tipped her chin. "That's good, because I want to kiss you." Reggie leaned up on her toes and pressed her lips to his.

He captured the back of her head in his hand and kissed her hard, his lips sealing hers, his tongue thrusting between her teeth. When he broke it off for air, his body was on fire, desire burning brighter than any flame.

"If we're sleeping here tonight, we better get cracking." He grabbed one of the sleeping bags and unrolled it.

Reggie, still wearing the towel tucked in at her breast, took the other end and pulled it straight, unzipping the bag to spread it out on the floor in front of the fire.

The house was cool everywhere but in front of the fireplace and getting colder as the weather settled in around the house. Snow fell so hard and fast, they couldn't see out past the porch. For all intents, they were cut off, isolated from the rest of the world.

Angus couldn't think of any better way to spend the evening than lying in front of a fire with Reggie lying beside him.

Once the bags were positioned, Reggie stared across at him, her eyes as bright as the flames. Giving the towel a gentle tug, she let it drop to the floor and stood with her shoulders back, her body bathed in the orange glow of the fire, the flickering flames casting dancing shadows over her smooth, soft skin.

With the grace of a cat, she stretched out on the sleeping bag and held out her hand.

"I don't know what I did to deserve you." Angus lowered himself to the floor beside her.

She laughed. "I hope you mean that in a good way."

"In the best way imaginable."

Reggie reached out and unstrapped his prosthetic and slipped it off his leg. She managed to make even that movement sexy. When she leaned over to set it aside, out of their way, he captured her hips and pulled her back against his front, cupping her breasts in his hands. "When we wake in the morning, promise me you'll have no regrets."

She turned in his arms and removed his towel from around his hips. "No regrets."

Angus had only one regret—he hadn't been completely honest with Reggie about why he was at the ranch. Now was the time for full disclosure. "Reggie, you should know—"

"Shh. Enough talk." She pressed her lips to his, cutting off his attempt at a confession.

Time enough to confess his role as a ranch hand and bodyguard in the morning. Tonight, he wanted to be with her.

Chapter Sixteen

Reggie woke before Angus, wrapped in his warm, strong arms, feeling more secure and protected than she had in a very long time.

Easing away from his body, she stared down at him, loving the hard angles of his face and the dark stubble on his jaw. She would love waking up to that face every day for the rest of her life. But neither one of them had spoken of anything past last night.

She really didn't know much about Angus, other than he was a good man, fearless and determined to protect her no matter the danger to himself. She shivered at the thought. The little tree she'd clung to had barely enough root dug into the cracks between the rocks to sustain her weight much longer. Had he left, she'd be dead, meeting a fate similar to Ted's.

At the thought of Ted, her heart squeezed in her chest. She'd loved her husband with all her heart. And yet, making love to Angus had felt so right.

Ted wouldn't have expected her to live the rest of her life alone. She wished she could talk to him. Tell him about Angus and ask for his approval. But Ted was gone.

That hadn't stopped her from visiting his grave and asking his advice before. When she'd been in doubt over decisions she'd had to make that he'd been primarily responsible for in the past, she'd gone to Fool's Fortune to the little cemetery where he'd been buried and asked his advice. Just talking to him had helped her to untangle her thoughts and make peace with the choices she made.

Leaving Angus asleep on the pallet of sleeping bags, Reggie rose and hurried down the hall to her bedroom where she dressed in warm clothing. A quick glance through the windows confirmed the snow had stopped falling and the wind had died down, but the clouds still hung gray over the landscape.

A fresh foot of snow blanketed the ground. Nothing she couldn't navigate in her truck. She'd done it hundreds of times. As long as it was snow, her tires would have the traction they needed to get her to town and back. She'd stop at the cemetery for a few minutes and then run by the diner to see if CW, Jo and Tad were still there. And then she'd stop by the Sheriff's office to report the incident at the ranch.

Until she made peace with Ted, she wouldn't

feel completely right about her affair with Angus or any other man.

Hell, just because she and Angus had made love three times didn't mean he wanted to take their relationship any further than it had gone. He might only be interested in sex without strings.

Though that wasn't Reggie's style, she couldn't fault him. He'd made no promises and neither had she.

With long underwear beneath her jeans, a long-sleeved shirt and sweatshirt over it, she pulled on thick wool socks and carried her boots through the living room to the back door.

Ranger followed her and sat on the tiled floor, watching her as she slipped her feet into her boots.

"I'll be back," she told the dog. "I just have to tie up some loose ends." Reggie pulled on her heavy winter coat, gloves and a stocking cap. Easing the back door open, she grabbed a scraper from a hook on the wall and stepped out into the snow that had been blown up on the porch.

She squinted at the morning sunshine glimmering off the glaringly white, virgin snow. Her truck was parked between the house and the barn, far enough out of listening range of the living room and her sleeping ranch hand.

In a few short minutes she had the snow and ice scraped from her windshield and was driving down the Last Chance Ranch's long driveway toward Fool's Fortune. The narrow road was covered in snow. When she reached the highway, she was relieved to see that a snowplow had already pushed the snow to the sides.

Reggie had no difficulty getting to town. Her biggest challenge had been leaving Angus. As she neared Fool's Fortune, she wondered what he'd think when he woke up and she was gone. Would he be disappointed or hurt, thinking she couldn't stand the idea of waking up with him? She couldn't help second-guessing her decision to leave him alone.

THE INCESSANT RINGING of a telephone pulled Angus out of a deep sleep. The deepest sleep he'd had since his injury. No nightmares about the enemy or finding members of his unit in pieces.

It took a moment for his eyes to adjust to the bright light streaming through the window. Then he realized he wasn't in a bed but on the floor of the living room of Reggie's house. The fire had died down to red coals and the lamp on the table beside the couch glowed brightly.

The electricity was back on.

He sat up and stared around. "Reggie?"

No answer. Perhaps she was in the bathroom in the back of the big house.

The phone, which had stopped ringing while he cleared the cobwebs from his brain, started ringing again. He scooted across the floor and reached for the phone.

"Davis residence."

"Ketchum?" Hank Derringer's voice came over the line.

"Yes, sir," Angus replied, surprised to hear his boss's voice on the telephone.

"How are things going in Colorado?"

"It's been a hell of a few days." Angus filled his boss in on the happenings on the Last Chance Ranch. "I just wish I knew who else was targeting her."

"I might have information on that front."

"Good. Shoot." With the phone receiver tucked between his ear and shoulder, Angus crawled back across the floor and strapped on his prosthetic leg.

"Of the names you gave me, Vance Peterson seems on the up-and-up."

"The speculator," Angus confirmed.

"He's from a hill-country town outside of San Antonio, Texas. Has a wife and daughter and no police record."

"Okay." Angus digested that. "What did you find on Freeman?"

"He's been in and out of trouble with the law for assault, arson and trespass. He's been known to make homemade bombs."

Angus pinched the bridge of his nose, wishing they'd been more successful holding on to the man once they'd caught him. "Nice to know. We caught Freeman sabotaging the livestock. When we stopped him for questioning, he admitted he'd been paid to scare Ms. Davis."

"By who?" Hank asked.

"He got away before we could get that information out of him." Angus's chest tightened at the memory of Reggie clinging to the side of the cliff. One tree root away from death.

"Brandon couldn't find anything on Lillian Kuntz. Including the fact she didn't have a registered driver's license in the state of Colorado. With nothing to go on, he pulled up the real estate photo of Lillian Kuntz and ran facial recognition software on her and got a hit."

"And?"

"Lillian Kuntz, aka Linda Kissinger, aka Lidia Kane." Hank paused. "The woman has a rap sheet the length of my arm. She's served time for embezzlement, bank fraud, extortion, welfare fraud, Ponzi schemes—you name it. Every time she's arrested, she's been let out on bail. And that's the last they see of her until she's caught again. She runs, changes her name and starts all over in her new life committing similar crimes in different locations."

"Great."

"While I was at it, I ran a scan on the other partner in her and Reggie's brother's real estate agency."

"Find anything on him?"

"Not really. He's got a business license in construction and also has a small mining business himself. Something to be aware of...he has access to explosives."

"Explosives?"

"The kind used in mining."

Once Angus had his leg in the device, he pushed to his feet. "Sounds like someone is looking for gold."

"That's the other thing we discovered," Hank continued. "Brandon took the photo of the old map and overlaid it with a contour map of the area. First of all the directional arrow was completely opposite of where it should have been. Rotating the map one-hundred-eighty degrees, it fit right over the Lucky Lady and the Last Chance ranches. Based on the contour map, satellite overlays and the old map overlay, the X marks the position of a ranch house. Based on the land plat, the house is where Ms. Davis lives."

Angus nearly dropped the phone. "The ranch house?"

"That's right. Is there a mine near the house?"

"The house sits on a slight knoll. I haven't seen any signs of any excavation or mine tunnels near the house or the barn."

"Does the house have a basement?"

"It's a wine cellar."

"Could be what the attacker is looking for."

"I'll check it." Angus held the receiver, ready to drop it on the charger. "Anything else?"

"Not for now. Hope that helped. How's Ms. Davis?"

"I haven't seen her yet this morning."

"Given how many attempts have been made on her life, you better find her."

"Agreed. I'll let you know what I find out about the basement, if I find anything."

"Do I need to send additional CCI personnel?"

"It would take too long. If I need help, I'll call in the local law enforcement."

"We're on standby if you should need us. I can fly men up there in hours," Hank assured him.

"Thanks, Mr. Derringer. For the opportunity and for believing in me."

"I consider myself a good judge of character. And you've got a good reputation. I only hire the best." Hank rang off.

Angus set the phone in the charger and hurried to the back of the house, calling out, "Reggie!"

Her room and bathroom were empty. She could have gone out to check on the animals.

As soon as he had on his jeans, shirt and boots, he threw his jacket on and stepped outside. Ranger was at his heels.

Outside the house, snow covered the ground. A set of footprints led to where Reggie's truck had been the night before. Tire tracks told the rest of the story. Reggie had left.

How could he have slept through her departure?

Angus returned to the house and grabbed the cordless phone, punching Reggie's cell number into the keypad.

After the fifth ring, he returned the receiver to the charger.

Angus put Ranger in his kennel, hurried out of the house to his truck and then slid into the driver's seat, a knot forming in his gut. He just knew something was wrong. The longer he took, the less likely he would be to find Reggie in time.

In time for what, he wasn't sure.

REGGIE DROVE STRAIGHT to the cemetery, determined to get a load off her chest and free her mind of any guilt concerning her dead husband and her newfound feelings for the ranch hand.

The road crew had cleared the main highways and roads, but the back road to the cemetery was still packed with snow. As she turned the corner onto the street leading to the graveyard, the back end of her truck fishtailed. She eased off the gas until the truck righted.

Parking on the side of the street, she sat for a moment, staring out at the pristine landscape, fresh with newly fallen snow, untouched by human feet or hands. Marble gravestones jutted out of the drifts. Chase's great-great-great-grandmother's stood the tallest, as if Lady Jones still flaunted her wealth to the descendants of the town who surely would have snubbed a former prostitute.

Each time she'd come to visit Ted, she'd felt a sense of calm wash over her. Perhaps it was the silence of the cemetery or the fact it was set a little way out from the rest of the town on a gentle hill. A beautiful setting for eternal rest. In the winter, the gravestones and the snow gave the cemetery a monochromatic tone. Black, white and a multitude of shades of gray.

Reggie dropped down from the truck, her boots sinking into a foot of snow. She tromped up to the wrought-iron gate, brushed the snow away with her foot and pulled it open.

Ted's grave was on the fourth row to the south, near a giant blue spruce tree. On the stone she'd had written, "Beloved husband and father."

Tad had been a good man, a loving husband and he'd loved his son deeply.

Reggie's eyes stung as she stared down at the stone. The fake flowers she and Tad had brought out last fall stuck out of the snow an inch, the bright pink-and-red silk roses a garish splash of color in an otherwise stark palette.

Reggie plucked the flowers from the snow, shook off the flakes and held the bouquet in her hand.

"Hi, Ted. I'm sorry I haven't been to visit in a couple months. You know how busy we get on the ranch. And with you gone, I'm having a time of keeping up with everything."

She sucked in a deep breath, her throat aching with tears. "Tad's getting bigger. It won't be long before he learns to ride and help out with the animals. You'd be very proud of him. He's well mannered and has a big heart. Just like you."

A single tear slipped from the corner of her eye. She brushed it away with her hand and stared down at the faded flowers.

"I didn't think I'd ever care about someone else after you died." Another tear fell and she wiped it from her cheek, but others followed and soon she gave up. "At first, I missed you so badly I could barely make my feet move." Her voice dropped to a whisper. "But lately, not as much."

Swallowing hard on the lump choking her throat, she pushed on. "Thing is, I want to have a life. To find someone to love me and to love again. I have enough love in my heart to remember you and to love another, whether it's the ranch hand or someone else.

"I wish you could meet Angus." She chuckled, though it sounded more like a sob. "He's a one-legged cowboy, but he's strong enough on one leg, you'd never know. And he's kind. He's patient with Tad and he saved my life. Twice."

She ducked her head, plucking at the red rose. "If it's okay with you… I'd like to get to know him better."

Reggie stared at the headstone. "I'll never forget you, Ted. Never." She stood for a long moment. Whether she waited for a sign from her dead husband or what, she didn't know. It just felt right to stand there in the silence.

When the cold seeped through the thickness of her jacket, she pushed the flowers into the ground and turned to leave. On a branch of a tree, a lone gray dove perched, his little eyes staring straight at Reggie. After a moment the bird spread its wings and flew upward.

The bird rose into the sky. Reggie's spirits rose with it. "Thanks, Ted."

She climbed into her truck and drove toward the diner. As she approached the edge of town, she spotted a sleek, pearl-white SUV on the side of the road to the south. As she turned north, Reggie glanced in her rearview mirror at the vehicle.

A man in a dark coat stood on the driver's side, talking to the person at the wheel. Beside him was a camouflage four-wheeler much like the one Daniel Freeman had driven the day before up in the hills.

Reggie's heart skipped several beats. She removed her foot from the accelerator and studied the man. If it was Freeman, she could hurry to the sheriff and report what he'd done. With the phone system out the night before, she'd have thought the man would make a run for it and get the hell out of town.

The man lifted his head.

Her pulse pounding, Reggie recognized that face. It was Freeman. She hesitated. Would she be better off going straight to the sheriff or following Freeman so that he couldn't get away?

Freeman left his ATV and climbed into the pearl-white SUV on the passenger side.

Her stomach turning flip-flops, Reggie eased down a side road between houses and parked in the first driveway.

A car and a dark truck passed, headed toward the cemetery. So intent on spotting the SUV coming from the direction she'd just traveled, she didn't note the makes or models of either of the passing vehicles, nor who was driving them.

When the SUV drove by, Reggie got a clear view of the driver.

Lillian Kuntz. What was she doing with Daniel Freeman?

Reggie dug her cell phone out of her purse and turned it on. She rarely used it since there was little reception out at the ranch. But in town it had three bars of service. She dialed her brother's number as she backed out of the driveway and pulled onto the road well behind Lillian's vehicle.

"Fool's Fortune Real Estate, William Coleman speaking."

"Will?"

"Reggie? Is everything all right?"

"That's what I want to know." The vehicle in front of her turned at a corner two blocks away. Reggie slowed and turned when she reached the same corner. The street they'd turned onto was also the highway that led out of town.

"What do you mean?" Will said.

"Are you and Lillian still engaged?"

He paused. "Why do you ask?"

"I just saw her drive away with Daniel Freeman, the man who's been causing trouble out at the Last Chance Ranch."

"Freeman was the one sabotaging you?"

"Yes."

Her brother's jaw tightened. "I knew she was up to something."

"Oh, William." Her heart ached for her brother. "What happened?"

"I don't know. Ever since we visited the ranch yesterday, she's been acting distant. It started in the basement."

"The basement? Did I miss something?"

"Remember? We went to the wine cellar to find a bottle of champagne to celebrate our engagement."

Had that only been yesterday? She'd almost died yesterday. That seemed so much more catastrophic than an argument in the wine cellar. "What got her panties in a twist?"

"I picked a bottle of wine. When I turned

around to show her, she was at the back of the cellar pulling wine bottles off a rack. When I asked her what she was doing, she got mad and accused me of being too nosy and controlling. That's why we left the house in such a hurry. She stormed out. On the way back to town, she broke off the engagement, claiming she couldn't be with a man who didn't trust her."

"Wow. The woman is crazy."

"I thought it was me. Something I said or did." Her brother snorted. "I went over and over in my mind what had happened in the wine cellar and came to the same conclusion you did. The woman is nuts and I dodged a bullet when she broke it off."

"Well, I'm behind her and she appears to be headed out of town on the highway that leads to the Last Chance Ranch. Is there any property she's been showing out that way?" The Lucky Lady and the Last Chance ranches weren't the only places on that road.

"I wouldn't think she'd show Freeman any-thing. The man doesn't have two nickels—rub—gether." Her brother's voice crackled and broke up.

As she left town the reception on her cell phone dropped quickly.

"Gotta go."

"Reg—"

The line went dead. A glance at the reception

indicator showed No Service. Reggie lifted her foot from the accelerator. Should she go back to town and let someone know what she was doing?

If Lillian and Daniel were headed out to the ranch, Angus was there for backup.

Staying well behind the pearl-white SUV, she followed the pair all the way out to the entrance to the Last Chance.

The SUV turned off just short of the drive leading up to the ranch, pulling onto a side road and parking behind trees.

Reggie slowed to a stop and waited a few minutes before easing up to where she'd last seen the SUV. The SUV sat tucked into the bushes and trees overhanging the road. Only it was empty of all persons.

Reggie pulled in behind the SUV and parked her truck. She climbed down and walked toward the empty SUV. A trail of fresh footprints led away from the vehicle headed directly to her house.

Why would Lillian and Daniel go in on foot unless they were planning more sabotage to her home or family?

Anger spiked and Reggie ran for her truck. If Angus was still asleep, he could be in danger. Even if he wasn't asleep, he wouldn't be expecting an attack.

Chapter Seventeen

Angus figured he wasn't far behind Reggie. His first stop in town was the diner. Inside he found Kitty at the counter, pouring coffee.

"Angus, good to see you." Kitty's smile filled the room. "Do you want a table of your own or are you joining CW, Jo and Tad?"

Glancing around at a corner booth, he spied the trio.

Tad jumped up and ran at him, full-force, slamming into his knees, hugging him tightly and nearly knocking him off his feet. "Mr. Angus, are you having breakfast with us?"

"I'd love to another time. Right now I'm looking for your mother."

CW rose from the table, leaving his half-eaten breakfast. "You lost Ms. Davis?"

"She slipped out of the house this morning before I woke up." He didn't tell him that he'd slept on the floor with her naked, or that they'd made love until late into the night. He didn't think CW had had that in mind when he'd asked Hank Derringer to send a bodyguard out to protect his boss.

"You think she's in town?"

"She took her truck. The tracks in the snow lead to the highway. I could only assume she came to town for something."

"Did you try the feed store or the hardware store?"

With a nod Angus answered, "I drove past them and didn't see her truck."

"What about the bank or the grocery store?"

Angus shook his head.

"Not there, either?" CW scratched his chin.

Kitty set the coffeepot on the burner and wiped her hands on her apron. "If she came to town and didn't need supplies, she's probably looking for advice about something."

"What do you mean?" Angus asked.

Kitty tipped her head, "I saw the way she looked at you the other day. She's attracted to you."

Angus's neck burned and the heat rose into his cheeks.

"And from the look on your face and the worry in your voice, I can only guess that you have feelings for our girl." Kitty crossed her arms over her chest. "Am I right?"

"Reggie's a special woman," Angus conceded.

"You got that right," Kitty said. "And she's

loving and loyal to a fault. Right now, she's probably carrying a whole lot of guilt for having feelings for anyone but you know who." Kitty's gaze skimmed over Tad.

"Tad, honey, go finish your pancakes," Jo said, turning him toward the table.

"If Mamma's lost, I want to help Mr. Angus find her."

Angus smiled down at the little boy. "She's not lost. We just don't know where she went. Like when you sneak out of the house to go to the barn. You're not lost, are you?"

He shook his head. "No."

"But your mother wouldn't always know where you went, right?"

The boy nodded. "Mamma's not lost?"

"No. She knows where she is."

"Okay." Tad glanced around at the faces of the adults. "Then I'll finish my pancakes." He hurried back to the table and dug into the syrupy treat.

"Like I was saying," Kitty continued. "She's probably feeling guilty for liking someone other than Ted."

Jo nodded. "I bet I know where she went."

CW, Kitty and Angus all turned to the older woman.

"She visits the graveyard where Ted was buried when she needs advice." Jo's eyes misted.

"She's been going there at least once a month since he passed."

"Think she'd go there in the snow?"

"It never stopped her before." Jo glanced at Angus. "And if she's thinking of moving on, she has even more of a reason to talk to Ted."

Ready to look anywhere, Angus asked, "Where?"

"On the road leading out the south side of town. There's a little church and a gated cemetery beside it," CW said. "You can't miss it."

"I'm going to check. If I don't find her, I'll head back to the house. I might have missed her on my way into town."

"We'll wrap it up here and head out to the house, as well," Jo said. "We were almost done anyway."

"Is Reggie in trouble?" Kitty asked.

"She could be." Angus had a gut feeling she'd be in big trouble if they didn't find her quickly. "I tried calling her when I got into town, but she's not answering her cell."

"Have you tried the ranch? She might have gotten back already?"

"I didn't pass her on the way in," Angus said.

Kitty glanced toward the window. "If I see her, I'll get her to stay put until one of you come for her."

"Good."

"Let me know when you find her. She's my best friend. I don't know what I'd do without her."

Angus almost responded with, "Me, too," but he bit down on his tongue before he could. It wasn't possible to be so attached to a woman when he'd only known her a couple days. Was it?

An image of her lying naked beside him, bathed in the glow from the fireplace, rose in his mind and made his heart swell with something he'd never felt before.

Sure, he'd had his share of relationships prior to his injury. But none that had lasted past the second date. He'd never found a woman who commanded his respect and admiration quite like Reggie. But what he felt was more than respect and admiration. Everything about her drew him to her and made him want to be with her, to hold her and become part of her tight circle of friends and family.

She was the real deal. And he couldn't wait to get her back in his sights. The longer she was away from him, the more he feared she was in danger.

He drove the short distance to the cemetery, searching for Reggie's truck along the way. At one point he thought he saw it, but it was parked in a residential driveway on a side street. He hadn't asked Kitty or the Reinhardts if she had friends she visited in Fool's Fortune.

Rather than stop to check it out, he'd pushed on to the graveyard where he hoped to find her talking to her dead husband.

When he passed the little church, his optimism plummeted. Yes, there were tire tracks in the fresh snow and even footprints.

Angus got out of the truck and trudged through the snow, opening the gate to the cemetery. The footprints led directly to a headstone with the name Theodore Alan Davis written in bold letters.

Jo had been right. Reggie had come to talk to her husband. What advice had she sought from the dead man? What decisions had she walked away with? And, damn it, he was worried about her.

Too worried to stay and contemplate her need to converse with her husband, Angus hurried back to his truck. Maybe that had been her truck on the street he'd passed.

He hurried back to where he'd seen it, but it was gone. She wasn't at any of the usual places on his way through town. He could have missed her altogether and she might be on her way to the Last Chance.

CW's truck still sat in front of the diner. Which meant, if Reggie reached the ranch before them, she'd be alone. If Daniel Freeman or the person who'd hired him wanted to get to her, they'd have the perfect opportunity while the rest of the family and the ranch hand were in town. From the information Hank had passed on, Lillian Kuntz seemed the most likely suspect.

Angus hurried through town. When he reached the highway heading to the ranch, he pressed his left foot to the accelerator and sped across the snow-crusted road toward the Last Chance Ranch, praying he was being overly paranoid and that he wasn't too late.

REGGIE FOLLOWED THE tracks toward the ranch house, wishing she had the rifle Angus had carried with them yesterday. It was probably where they'd left it in the barn, hanging over the door of the tack room.

Reggie hurried forward, more concerned about Angus. If he was still asleep, he wouldn't have time to fit his leg in the prosthetic. He could be helpless on the floor of the living room.

She snuck up behind the barn. The footprints led directly to the back of the house. A quick glance around the barnyard and the house reassured her.

All the vehicles were gone, including Angus's truck. That left her and the two people headed toward her house.

Reggie slipped in through the back door of the barn. In the tack room she removed the rifle from where it hung over the door, loaded rounds into the weapon and shot the bolt home. Feeling better able to face Lillian and Dan Freeman, she slipped out the back door of the barn and crossed the barnyard to the house.

She heard the muffled sound of a dog barking. Angus must have left Ranger at the house, confined to his kennel.

Careful to avoid squeaky boards, she eased her way up on the back porch and peered through the windows into the kitchen. The room was empty and the door to the cellar stood open. She tried the kitchen door handle. It was locked. Afraid using her key on the back door would alert the trespassers, she moved around the porch to the front of the house. A glance through the living room window proved that room was empty, as well.

The barking grew louder as she approached the window to the bedroom Angus used. The dog obviously knew something wasn't right and wanted out to investigate. Reggie prayed the barking would cover the sound of her opening the front door. She inserted her key and twisted. Once the dead bolt was unlocked, she pushed the door open slowly with the barrel of the rifle.

No one stood on the other side and the living room to her left was still empty. Leaving the door open, she slipped down the hallway, tiptoeing on the hardwood flooring, wondering if she should remove her boots.

Her bedroom was empty. She checked the

bathroom and under the bed, just in case, then moved back to the hallway. Ranger had stopped barking. When she entered the room, he whined and scratched at the welded-wire door of the kennel.

Reggie released the lock and opened the door. Ranger might not be human, but he was more backup than nothing. As soon as the door swung open the dog leaped out and headed for the hallway. "Heel," Reggie whispered sharply.

Ranger halted so fast, his toenails skidded on the wood. He looked down the hallway and whined again, a low growl rumbling in his chest.

"I know. They don't belong here," Reggie whispered. A quick search of the other rooms in the house came up empty. Then she heard muffled voices...as if they came from beneath the floor.

The cellar door had been open. They had to be down there. But why? Surely they hadn't come to steal bottles of wine.

Reggie worked her way slowly to the top of the cellar stairs and paused, listening.

"Put your back into it." Lillian's voice echoed against the stone walls of the basement. "The door has to be behind that wine rack."

"If you want it moved, put your back into it, as well." Daniel Freeman's voice carried to where Reggie stood.

Ranger's chest rumbled with a low growl.

Reggie tapped his nose softly and looked into the dog's eyes as she whispered, "No."

The shepherd's ears flattened and the need to go after the people in the basement caused his body to shake.

"Empty the damned thing and it'll be easier to move. For the love of Mike, we don't have all day," Lillian said. The crashing, splashing sound of full bottles of wine hitting the stone floor filled the air.

Reggie's hands curled around the handle of the rifle, her lips curling back in a snarl. Her husband might have been a rancher, but he and his father before him had collected wine for years. There were very expensive bottles on those racks and it sounded as if they were being destroyed.

Reggie bit down hard on her tongue to keep from yelling for the two to stop trashing her wine cellar. Instead she eased down the stairs, the crashing bottles masking her descent into the cellar.

The noise stopped.

"Now we can move it," Freeman said. A loud scraping sound grated against Reggie's ears.

"There it is," Lillian said. "It's sealed shut."

"I've got this," Freeman bragged.

"Hurry. They could be home anytime," Lillian said.

Curious about what they were up to, Reggie squatted on the steps halfway down and glanced across the rows of wine racks. She made out the tops of Lillian's and Freeman's heads.

Freeman was pressing something into the side of what looked like a steel panel welded to a metal frame on the back wall.

"It's set." Freeman stepped back. "We have five minutes to get out before it blows."

Reggie's heart skipped several beats and then raced ahead. Blows? From the sound of it, Freeman had set an explosive charge on the back wall.

"Correction," Lillian said, her voice as cold as the stone walls of the cellar. "*I* have five minutes to get out of here before it blows."

Freeman turned toward Lillian. "What the hell?" His hands rose to where Reggie could see them over the racks. "Point that thing somewhere else. It's liable to go off."

"That's the idea." A shot blasted through the air.

Reggie gasped.

Freeman slipped to the ground without another word.

Lillian turned and headed back through the rows of wine bottles toward the stairs.

Frozen in the crouched position, Reggie didn't move soon enough.

When Lillian appeared at the end of the first row, a smile curled her lips, and the pistol in her hand leveled on Reggie.

"Oh, good. I can take care of you while you're here. I suggest you march your manly boots down here and face me."

"So you can kill me like you killed Freeman?"

"That's the plan."

"Sorry to spoil your little plan." Clutching the rifle to her side, Reggie leaped down the side of the staircase to the stone floor and rolled.

A shot rang out, sparks bounced up next to Reggie, missing her completely and giving her the chance to dive behind the first shelf of wine bottles.

"Now be a good little tomboy and stand still while I kill you," Lillian called. Another shot rang out and a bottle of wine exploded above Reggie's head, splattering over her.

She kept still and low to the ground. Through the wooden stands holding bottles of wine, Reggie peered. She could only see the woman's legs, encased in smart wool-blend trousers and shapely snow boots. Dark spots marred the fabrics from blood or wine. Reggie couldn't tell and really didn't want to know.

She slipped her rifle through one of the gaps and lay low, lining up her sites, waiting for Lillian to step in range.

A leg appeared at the end of her site.

Reggie squeezed the trigger.

Lillian screamed and fell to the ground. Her

gun hit the floor, sliding across the surface of the stone. Reggie darted out of her hiding place.

The sound of boots pounding against the floor above made her pulse pound faster. Did Lillian have anyone else working for her? Or had CW and Angus arrived?

Lillian lay on the floor by the stairs, clutching at a wound on her calf. "You shot me!"

"Yeah, and I'd do it again. You killed a man and wrecked my cellar." Reggie pointed her rifle at Lillian. "And from what Freeman said, I'm betting you're the one who paid him to cause me all the trouble."

"If you'd sold it, I wouldn't have had to pay Freeman to scare you off the land."

"Is that what you were doing?" Reggie shook her head. "If you knew anything about me, you'd know nothing was going to get me off this land. Nothing."

"That's where you're wrong." Lillian's eyes narrowed as she pulled herself up on the stair railing.

"You can stop right there," Reggie warned the other woman, leveling her rifle on her.

"Or what? You'll shoot me again?" Lillian shook her head. "Go ahead, but you'll have to shoot me in the back. And if I know you, you won't." She limped up one step, blood dripping from the wound on her calf. Then she pulled herself up to the next step and another.

Reggie followed her, holding her rifle in front of her.

Lillian fell against the stairs and moaned.

Angry at all Lillian had done to hurt her, Reggie hesitated. "Lillian?"

When the woman didn't answer, Reggie edged closer to the inert form.

A whir of motion caught her off guard.

Lillian swung out her arm and knocked the rifle from Reggie's grasp. "I'll have this ranch, damn you." The woman pushed to her feet.

Reggie stood tall, ready to take the woman down with her bare hands. "No, you'll be off my ranch and in a jail cell by the end of the day."

"Sorry, sweetheart, that's not part of my plan. I have exactly—" she glanced down at her watch "—two minutes to get out of here. And you aren't coming with me." Nearing the top of the stairs, she reached behind her, pulled out a small pistol and aimed it at Reggie's chest. "The house is wired to explode and you're going up with it."

"Not if I have anything to say about it." Angus appeared behind Lillian.

Angus grabbed for Lillian.

Her pistol went off.

Chapter Eighteen

Angus yanked Lillian's arm up behind her, forcing her to drop the pistol. The woman kicked and fought, but he pushed her arm up the middle of her back harder and wrapped his other arm around her neck, holding her tight until she quit struggling.

When he glanced down at Reggie, she lay at the bottom of the stairs, her hand pressed to her thigh.

"Mamma?" a child's voice called out behind Angus.

"Tad!" Jo called from somewhere behind him. "Tad, get back here."

Angus's heart stopped. He couldn't let go of Lillian, for fear she'd attack Reggie again and he couldn't get to Reggie unless he let go of Lillian.

"Get Tad out of the house. Now!" Reggie screamed. "There are explosives set to go off in thirty seconds. Go!"

Angus dragged Lillian up the remaining steps.

CW was behind him, carrying a shotgun.

Angus shoved Lillian at the older man. "Shoot her if she tries anything. Get out of the house, now! It's set to explode. Jo, get Tad as far away from the house as you can. Go! Go! Go!"

CW gripped the arm Angus had shoved up between Lillian's shoulder blades and pushed the woman toward the back door. Jo and Tad rushed out ahead of them.

Angus held on to the stair rail and ran as fast as he could down the stairs.

Reggie was pulling herself up by the railing. "Get out."

"Not without you," Angus argued.

He looped her arm over his shoulder and started up the stairs with her.

"Leave me and save yourself."

"Quit arguing and get up the stairs and we'll both live."

"Damned stubborn man."

"Hardheaded woman."

Together, they pushed through the cellar door into the kitchen.

A quick dive for the back door and they were out on the porch and down the stairs.

The explosion started in the belly of the house. A rumble was followed by the world shattering around them.

Angus shoved Reggie face-first into the snow and threw himself over her body.

Rocks, boards, splinters and rubble shot out in all directions, pummeling his back and extremities. When the first round settled, Angus dared to look up.

"Are you okay?" he asked.

"Yeah."

She didn't look okay, but he didn't have time to question her. Once a house exploded, if a gas line ruptured it could cause a residual explosion and subsequent fire. They had to get as far away from the house as possible.

Angus lurched to his good foot and steadied himself. Then he reached for Reggie's hand.

He pulled her to her feet and then lifted her into his arms.

"I can walk."

"You're bleeding...losing blood." Phantom pain chose that moment to shoot up his leg like a dozen stabbing knives. Angus grit his teeth and pushed forward, aiming for the barn. If he could just get her to the other side of the barn...

As he reached the barn, another explosion rocked the earth beneath him. He stumbled, but remained upright, still carrying Reggie. A fireball of flame rose up behind him, sending out a heated glow, warming his back.

Angus didn't stop until he reached the back of the barn. CW had tied Lillian up with a horse's lead rope. He handed the shotgun to Jo and hurried over to help Angus lower Reggie to the ground.

"I'm fine." Reggie's voice lacked its usual strength and determination and her face had lost much of its color. Despite her words to the contrary, the wound on her leg bled profusely.

Angus had to slow or stop the flow of blood or she'd bleed out before they got her to a hospital. He pulled off his belt and wrapped it around her thigh above the wound, slipped the end through the buckle and pulled until it dented the skin. Immediately the bleeding slowed. Angus shrugged out of his jacket and wrapped it around Reggie to keep her from going into shock.

"You're gonna get cold." Reggie tried to hand him his coat.

"Keep it." He tugged his shirt out of his waistband, removed it and then tore it into strips. Once he'd folded a single strip into a square pad, he pressed it to her wound. He shot a glance at CW. "Keep pressure on it."

The older man's face was pale, but he dropped to the ground beside Reggie and held the pad firmly against her leg.

Angus took another strip and tied it around her leg, securing the knot over the pad before CW removed his hand.

"Hey," Lillian shouted. "What about me? I'm bleeding over here."

Angus handed the rest of his shirt strips to Jo.

The older woman wrapped a strip of fabric around Lillian's leg and knotted it with enough pressure to make the woman squeal. "You're lucky I don't just let you bleed out. No one hurts our Reggie," Jo said in a tone low enough not to disturb Tad.

Angus had heard and couldn't have agreed with Jo more.

"Is Mamma gonna die?" Tad stood beside Reggie, his face pale, his bottom lip trembling.

"No, Tad," Angus said. "She's going to be fine. Aren't you, Reggie?"

She reached out to Tad and cupped his chin. "That's right, sweetie. I'm gonna be fine. I'm just going to take a little nap." Reggie closed her eyes. "Just a nap."

His gut clenching, Angus reached down to lift Reggie. "Help me get her into the truck."

CW helped him lift Reggie into his arms. The old man ran ahead of him and opened the back door to Angus's truck. Ranger jumped down.

Angus gave the dog the command, "Stay."

Ranger sat on his haunches in the snow and watched as CW and Angus stretched Reggie out on the backseat.

"CW, you stay here with the woman. I'll send the sheriff and an ambulance when I get to town."

"Tad and I are going with Ms. Reggie," Jo said, refusing to let Angus say otherwise.

"Good. I want you to drive while I stay with her. Tad will have to sit in the front seat."

They shifted Tad's booster seat to the front, loaded up and headed for Fool's Fortune. As soon as they were within range of a cell tower, Angus placed an emergency call.

A sheriff's deputy was dispatched along with a fire truck to the ranch.

At Fool's Fortune's small trauma center, Reggie was immediately taken into surgery.

Once Reggie was wheeled away, Angus got on the phone with Hank, filling him in on what had happened.

"That was far too close. I'm sorry. I didn't realize the job would be as dangerous as it turned out. I wouldn't have asked you to take on such an undertaking."

"Sir." Angus stopped his boss. "I'm glad you sent me."

"Why?"

"A really wonderful woman might not be alive today had I not been here. And it proved to me that I'm not washed up."

"Far from it, from the sound of it. You're a great addition to Covert Cowboys Inc."

"About that…"

"Let me guess. You want to stay in Colorado?"

"How'd you know?"

"I take it you want to stay on board and help Ms. Davis rebuild."

"Yes, sir. She's going to need all the help she can get."

"Even from a crippled cowboy?" Hank asked.

"That's right. Or, as she put it, a one-legged cowboy." Angus chuckled.

"She's okay with it?"

"Handled it better than I did."

"That Ms. Davis is special."

Angus's heart squeezed tight. "I know, sir."

"Give her my condolences over the loss of her home."

Angus paused. "I haven't actually told her about you or my assignment."

"That ought to raise her eyebrows. Think she'll be upset?"

"If she is, I'm man enough to handle it."

"Glad to hear it. And, Angus?"

"Yes, sir."

"When you're ready, I'll have more assignments for you."

"I'll let you know when I'm free to take on more work. In the meantime, I see the doc. Gotta go."

Angus shoved his cell phone into his pocket and met the doctor as he emerged from the door marked Restricted to Staff.

"How is she?" Angus asked.

"Are you a relative?"

Kitty had joined Jo and Tad in the waiting room while Angus had been on the phone.

"That would be us. We all want to know how our Reggie is."

The doctor glanced at the people standing around him. "Hospital regulations—"

"—be damned. How is Reggie?"

With a sigh, the doctor responded. "She's doing fine. I removed the bullet and cauterized the bleeders. She's weak, but she'll be okay and could probably go home in the morning."

Kitty smiled sadly. "Only she doesn't have a home anymore. She can stay with me, but my place is too small to take all of you."

"We'll stay at the Gold Rush Tavern," Angus stated. He didn't want to be that far away from Reggie. After all that had happened to her, she'd need someone to lean on and he planned to be there for her.

THREE DAYS LATER, Reggie stood in front of the charred barn, her arm hooked in Angus's as she leaned against him to keep most of her weight off her healing leg.

Angus had confessed his role as her bodyguard while she'd been recovering in her hospital bed. And, though she'd been shocked, it hadn't changed her feelings for him.

"I appreciate you sticking around after solving my case," she said.

"I'll stay as long as you want me." He covered

her hand with his. "Thanks for not being too angry with CW for hiring a bodyguard."

"Let him think I'm still mad. It'll do him good." She winked, her heart lighter than it had been in more than a year. "And remind me to thank him in a week or two."

"I will."

"The gold in the buried mine will make it easier for me to take care of Tad." She smiled. "I won't have to worry where the college money will come from, or how I'll pay for hay and feed for the cattle."

"You really won't have to raise cattle at all, if you don't want to."

Reggie nodded. "I know. But it's who I am. And I want Tad to know what it means to work hard and take care of others, including animals."

"You're a good mother."

"He's a good kid." She nudged Angus in the side. "Hey, you promised to teach him how to ride."

Angus nodded. "I will, and I bet he'll take to it like a natural, like he was born to it. He's got instinct like his parents."

"I meant to thank you for letting Ranger sleep with Tad. After losing his home…well…it helped him remain calm and centered."

The German shepherd glanced up when his name was mentioned, his tail sweeping the ground.

"Ranger's an amazing animal. He helped me get through rehab."

Reggie's heart swelled, happy that Angus had confirmed he'd be around for the next few months while she rebuilt. And if he meant it when he'd said *as long as she wanted him.* That would be a very long time.

She glanced up at the man who'd saved her life several times.

Angus stared at the backhoe and the bull-dozer working together to load the rubble of the burned-out house into the back of a dump truck to be hauled away to the dump.

Reggie sighed. "Ted and I made some good memories in that house."

"You haven't lost those memories. They'll always be in your heart."

"Very poetic for a former soldier."

He nodded. "I have good memories of the men who died in the explosion that claimed my leg. I'll never forget them. As a tribute to their sacrifice, I plan on living a long and happy life. They would have wanted me to."

"And Ted would have wanted me to be happy, as well." She slipped her hand into Angus's. "So, what do you think? With our luck, do we have a chance at happily-ever-after?" Reggie held her breath, wondering if she was asking too much too soon.

Angus squeezed her hand and then let go without saying a word.

Reggie's chest tightened, her eyes burning. She wanted him to want her, more than anything. Loyal, strong, brave; he was the kind of man she needed to stand at her side against the challenges she faced, ranching in the Rockies.

More than that, he reminded her that she was one hundred percent woman, with needs and desires.

"I think we've been very lucky. Or at least, I have been. I found you." His arm slid around her waist and he pulled her body close to his and stared down into her eyes. "We have a very good chance at happily-ever-after. As long as we're together."

* * * * *

LARGER-PRINT BOOKS!
GET 2 FREE LARGER-PRINT NOVELS PLUS
2 FREE GIFTS!

HARLEQUIN®

INTRIGUE
BREATHTAKING ROMANTIC SUSPENSE

HILP15

READERSERVICE.COM

Manage your account online!

- Review your order history
- Manage your payments
- Update your address

*We've designed the
Reader Service website
just for you.*

Enjoy all the features!

- Discover new series available to you,
  and read excerpts from any series.
- Respond to mailings and special
  monthly offers.
- Connect with favorite authors at
  the blog.
- Browse the Bonus Bucks catalog
  and online-only exculsives.
- Share your feedback.

Visit us at:
ReaderService.com

RS15